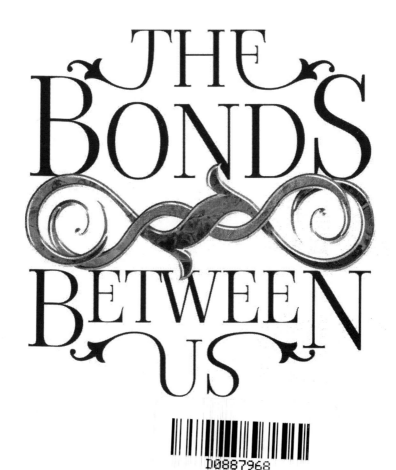

THE
BONDS
BETWEEN
US

BOOK ONE OF THE WEB OF WYRD TRILOGY

THE BONDS BETWEEN US

EMILY RUHL

atmosphere press

Published by Atmosphere Press

Cover design by Matthew Fielder

atmospherepress.com

This book is dedicated to my mom, whose endless love, patience, and unshakeable confidence in me mean more than words could ever say.

CHAPTER ONE

Venice was an enigma. A beautiful maiden all at once willing to flaunt her culture, wisdom, grace, and hospitality; yet at the same time, unpretentious, reserved, and shrouded by the mystery of her storied past. To most, she was an ambiguous acquaintance. But those who took the time to truly know her were rewarded with the gradual revelation of the more vulnerable and complex characteristics of her nature—a soul tinged with melancholy and insecurity, an existence fueled by a relentless spirit, and dark secrets concealed with cheery façades and formidable determination.

All things considered, La Serenissima and I had a lot in common. Perhaps that's what drew me to move here—a city halfway around the world from my original place of birth.

Now, Venice was my home. And I loved her dearly for

the solace and acceptance she had offered me. Moving here three years ago had been like finally finding clothes that fit properly—never before had I felt so much like I truly belonged somewhere. I knew without a doubt that this was where I was always meant to be.

And maybe Venice felt the same, judging by the secrets with which she suddenly seemed willing to entrust me. Secrets that no one else—at least no one willing to talk about them—appeared to know.

When I first started researching the city's myths as part of my next book, I thought it would be simple and straightforward. To instead find myself embroiled in a web of lies, clandestine patterns, and obfuscated details had been surprising. Every legend I discovered held similarities to others, the plots meshing almost perfectly together at some points. But there was always something missing, and I wasn't able to definitively connect the tales I read into a single cohesive story. Still, it was clear that there was more to the folklore than the mere passing along of lessons in morality by ancient, god-fearing Venetians. But what was it?

It was a mystery that had consumed my mind for *months*. Yet I felt no closer to the truth. It didn't help that my research was hindered by the deliberate eradication of any evidence that could be even remotely helpful. Pages had been ripped out of archaic tomes of Venetian folklore. There were inconsistencies in modern re-tellings of the myths. Even the simple acknowledgment of certain fables appeared to be taboo.

People were afraid—and they obviously had been for a very long time. But afraid of what? What was I missing?

And why did I have the unsettling feeling that

something ominous was lurking behind the answers to all of these questions?

Stepping out onto the stone street, these disquieting thoughts were driven from the front of my mind like a vampire from the sun. I blinked at the brightness of the outside world, my eyes having grown accustomed to the darkness of the library. Around me, the stone alleys and colorful palazzos were painted orange by the fiery glow of the setting sun. Slanting beams of light cascaded across tiled roofs, piercing the air as though making one final effort to stop the steadily dropping temperature.

I started down the narrow lane, tugging my jacket tighter around myself as a gust of wind whipped between the buildings. Cold tendrils of winter air slithered down my neck, and I hunched my shoulders against the unwelcome sensation. It was ironic, really, that I hated the cold so much... considering what I was. And perhaps if I was normal by any means, I'd have relished in the dark, cold, dampness of the winter months.

But I wasn't normal. I was an exception to the rule, as Giovanna was so fond of saying. She was my best friend, my sister in all but blood. Although I didn't always agree with her assessment of my character, I couldn't deny that she knew me better than anyone else. To her, it made perfect sense that I hated the winter—it was far too much a reminder of my past, and much too contrary to the warm heart she claimed I possessed. So, it certainly wouldn't have been surprising to her that as another frigid breeze rushed past me, I quickened my pace in my haste to return to the warmth of home.

It was difficult, though, to hurry through the crowded streets. For along with the colder weather that I disliked so much, December also brought more people—yet another thing I wasn't particularly fond of. I dodged and weaved through the masses of people loitering in the campi and alleys. Inhabitants of the city rushed home from work, holiday hoards milled in front of shop windows and cafés, tourists were taking pictures of... well, *everything*.

It was one of the downfalls of living in Venice. Granted, my list of complaints was short: the crowds and the traffic problems they created, tourists' general disrespect for the city, the rising cost of inhabiting even the smallest apartment, the flooding during the rainy season.

But still, the positives far outweighed the negatives. As a lover of the ocean, of course, one of the most appealing factors was the Floating City's ties to the sea. But I also loved everything that Venice had to offer on land—its charming architecture, its unique culture, its vibrant history...

Its location halfway around the world from my family.

I shook my head. Nope. I wasn't going down *that* path. It wouldn't do me any good to dwell on that now anyway.

Thump, thump.

I was startled from my swirling thoughts by something bumping against my leg. Glancing down, I spotted a soccer ball rolling near my foot. Stooping to pick it up, I turned in the direction of a squeaky "Scusa, signorina!" that echoed from across the campo. A young girl with white-blonde hair bounded toward me, her sheer energy carrying her across the cobblestone campo as though she was floating on air. She was flanked by several other children, following her in their quest to recover their run-away play item.

My lips twitched into a fond smile, and I tossed the ball

back to them. It bounced once, twice, and then the blonde girl caught it with a gleeful shout.

"Grazie!" came her enthusiastic reply before she turned and raced back toward her friends. I gave a slight wave in response, spinning around to continue on my way—

And crashed right into someone walking in the opposite direction.

I watched, horrified, as the scene before me played out in slow motion. The person—a young man who looked to be about my age—stumbled, arms flailing in his fight against gravity. At first, it looked like he might be successful in righting himself, but then he stumbled another step, tilted, and almost gracefully pirouetted in the air before tumbling to the ground with a soft *oomph*.

"Mi dispiace!" I exclaimed, hurrying forward to help him, my face heating up in embarrassment. "Sta bene?"

"Sì, sto a posto," he assured, pushing himself off the ground and dusting off his pants. Straightening, he adjusted the square, black-rimmed glasses that had been knocked askew on the bridge of his nose. As soon as his sight was restored, his gaze wandered to me. The moment his eyes met mine, my heart stuttered to a stop. They were breathtaking.

"La palla..." I began, clearing my throat and hoping that my voice sounded stronger to him than it did to my own ears. "Non L'ho visto."

"Va bene," he replied calmly, waving away my apology with a flourish of his hand. I must have looked skeptical, because he added softly, "Really, it's okay."

His shift from Italian to English momentarily startled me.

"How did you know I speak English?"

A small smile graced the stranger's lips.

"You speak Italian very well, but you have a slight American accent," he observed, his tone free of judgment.

"Ah. I hoped I was getting better at hiding it," I commented sheepishly.

An odd look crossed the stranger's eyes before he responded sagely, "I've always found that it's much better to stand out for being yourself, rather than to hide who you are just so that you can be like everyone else."

I gaped at him, too stunned to reply. How was it possible for a stranger to knock your world completely off-kilter with a single sentence? I had met this man less than five minutes ago, yet he had struck a sensitive chord deep within me. It was almost like he knew me, like he had seen into my soul with just one look and felt the need to heal the wounds he found there.

"So, are you here for the Festa di San Nicolò?"

I shook my head, though it was more to clear my mind than to answer his question.

"No. I live here."

"You do?"

"I moved here three years ago."

"Really? That's when I moved here, too!"

"You weren't born here?" I asked in surprise.

"No," he shook his head. "I'm originally from Fabbrico in Reggio Emilia."

"How did you end up here?"

"My brother and I are musicians," he explained. "When we first started our careers in Fabbrico, it was difficult to find work. There were very few jobs; and anyone who *was* hiring was only looking for experienced musicians, not amateurs. So, we had to start looking for work outside of Fabbrico. We were fortunate enough to find a few employers here who were willing to hire us."

"Do you miss Fabbrico?"

"Yes, at times. It was our childhood home." He shrugged. "But our parents are no longer there, either—they moved to Bologna to be near our sister when she started at university there. All that is left in Fabbrico are the memories. Venice is my home now, as well as my brother's. We are both very happy here."

He paused, tilting his head as he considered me. "But what about you? I know how *I* ended up here, but Fabbrico is a bit closer to Venice than the United States."

I smirked at the wry comment. "I studied abroad here when I was in college—spent a year at the Università Ca' Foscari Venezia studying history and modern languages. While I was there, I fell in love with Venice—with Italy. So, after I graduated, I decided to move here permanently."

"Did your family come with you?"

"No, they stayed in the States."

"You must miss them."

Such a simple, innocuous statement—yet it made me feel like I had just been punched in the gut.

Did I miss my family? I wasn't sure.

There were a few positive memories that I possessed from my youth, shining through the dark like stars in the night sky. But just like the night sky, most of my childhood, and especially my adolescence, had been a vast void of nothingness. I remembered cruel words, the malicious twisting of my actions to suit their perverse theories. I remembered being hidden, locked away. I remembered being abandoned by the people whose love I had yearned for all my life.

I definitely didn't miss any of *that*.

Still, a small part of me had always hoped that I might reconcile with my parents one day, and that I might be accepted back into our family with open arms. *That* was what I missed, more than anything else—the possibility of getting my family back again.

"It's complicated," I replied, cringing internally at the rather lame cliché. To be fair though, it was an accurate statement.

"Most things in life are." There it was—the opportunity to end this conversation. I could easily find a polite way to excuse myself and make a beeline back home. But, oddly enough, I didn't want to. There was something about this man that set me at ease, that drew me to him, that made me want to bare my soul to him.

Quite frankly, it was terrifying. I had spent years erecting walls around my heart. Yet here I was, ready to break them down for a person I met only five minutes ago.

His large doe eyes patiently watched me as I searched for the rights words to tell him enough—but not every-thing—to satiate his unspoken curiosity.

"I have a bit of a... *strained* relationship with my parents," I explained, already feeling far out of my comfort zone with that small admission. He seemed to sense my discomfort because he nodded and didn't press any further. But there was a glimmer of sadness in his eyes. And I hated it. Cold gloom didn't belong in those unusually warm brown depths. It had to disappear.

So, backpedaling a bit, I added brightly, "It's really not as bad as it sounds. Actually, when I relocated to Venice, I moved in with my best friend. We met in college. She's great. We're like sisters. She's my family here."

My words appeared to have their desired effect, as a small smile tugged at the stranger's lips.

"I'm glad to hear that," he said kindly. "What's her name?"

"Giovanna, but I would never call her that unless you want an hour-long lecture about everything she hates about the name. She's rather touchy about it."

"So, what *do* you call her?"

"Nina."

"Ah. And what about you?"

"Pardon?"

"What can I call you?"

"Oh!" I gasped as realization struck me. "I'm sorry! I probably should've mentioned that at some point, considering I plowed you over not ten minutes ago. I'm Katya." I extended my hand in greeting.

"Piacere, Katya." He embraced my hand with both of his in a firm, but gentle grasp. "I'm Matteo."

The moment our hands touched, an inexplicable warmth flooded through me, tingling through my veins. My gray eyes locked with his brown ones, and I was immediately sucked into their warm, dark depths. Looking into his eyes was like looking into his soul. Emotions danced in them like flickering flames. I easily identified joy, compassion, longing, sadness—but they flitted by so rapidly that I wasn't able to keep up. I was drowning in his eyes, in the sheer magnitude of the emotions that I was witnessing. They were so strong that I almost thought I could feel them myself.

I remained lost in his eyes, unable to look away even as the air was sapped from my lungs. Then, in a rare moment of boldness, my other hand came up to rest on his...

And the world gradually faded away. The buzz of the crowds around us dissipated. The buildings surrounding the campo blurred. Time slowed. Earth ceased spinning. My entire world shrank to a single point around which it revolved—and that point was Matteo.

Matteo, with his expressive chocolate eyes brimming with heartfelt emotion, his mouth stretching into a crooked smile that made my heart flutter, the steady warmth of his hands wrapped around mine.

I wasn't sure how long we stood there holding hands. The logical part of my mind insisted that it was only a few seconds. But in those few seconds, I felt like I had seen an eternity pass before me. My past and present merged. My future flashed across my mind like the reels of an old film. Generations preceding and following that sole instant slotted into place and stretched through the infinite expanse of time.

I wanted to stay there, in that moment with Matteo, forever. But it seemed that time had other plans. For at that moment, the bells of the clock tower began to toll—five deep, resonant chimes ringing across the square and echoing into the distance.

And just like that, the world snapped back into focus like a rubber band. The buildings around the perimeter of the Campo Santo Stefano were once again solid. The salty smell of the canals and the aroma of food from the nearby café filled the air. The hum of chatter, the peals of laughter, the lilting voices of the gondoliers all came rushing back. Time sped up, and the world resumed its steady rotations.

I reluctantly released my grip on Matteo's hands,

noticing with undisguised pleasure that he seemed equally as unwilling to part. When he did eventually let go of my hands, regret and pain flared briefly—but brightly—in his eyes before an indecipherable mask slipped across his features.

The separation caused an odd shift within me, as well. Along with the loss of physical contact came an internal emptiness, a coldness in my soul that had nothing to do with the weather. I felt peculiarly incomplete—as though a piece of myself was now missing.

"Well, us," Matteo coughed awkwardly. Apparently, he was just as flustered as I was. "As much as I've enjoyed talking with you, I'm afraid that's my cue to leave." He nodded in the direction of the campanile, which had now fallen silent. "I'm late for work."

"Oh, yes, of course. Sorry," I stammered. "I should be going, too." I moved to step around him. "It was nice meeting you, Matteo. Maybe we'll run into each other again one day."

"I hope we do—though perhaps not so literally."

I laughed. "Yeah, let's avoid that."

"Maybe we should plan our next meeting then. You know, to avoid injury." Matteo's lips twitched upward despite his attempt to keep a straight face.

"What did you have in mind?"

"How about the San Nicolò festival tomorrow? We could go together."

"Sure, I'd love to," I answered, conveniently ignoring the part of my mind that screamed at me to say no.

"Wonderful!" Matteo beamed. "I'll meet you here at this time tomorrow."

"Ok," I nodded. "A domani."

"Ciao," he bid in farewell, parting with a crooked smile and a wave. I remained frozen in place, watching as he crossed the campo.

Only when he had disappeared down an alleyway did I continue my own journey home. As my feet habitually carried me through alleys and across bridges, my mind drifted back to Matteo and our baffling meeting. Never before had I experienced anything even remotely similar to what had just transpired. I had absolutely no explanation for any of it. I had never met someone who stopped me in my tracks and consumed my entire world. Nor had I ever been so compelled to spill my heart and soul to someone. It was so uncharacteristic of me.

It left me to wonder...

What in the world had just happened?

CHAPTER TWO

The pleasant aroma of tomato sauce greeted me as I stepped through the door of the apartment. It was Nina's night to cook, which meant pasta was on the menu. She was rather... *selective* when it came to the food she ate, and one of the only dishes she would willingly and repeatedly consume involved pasta. On the nights when I cooked, I tried desperately to expand her palate and include at least a few healthier foods in her diet. Most of the time, I was successful. But as soon as Nina was in charge of dinner again, we were back to pasta.

Still, it was hard to be angry about it when Nina's pasta dishes were so delicious.

Taking a deliberate sniff of the air, I relished in the mouthwatering smell—

Wait.

My gaze darted to the pot on the stove, where thin

wisps of smoke were rising from the contents. Dropping my bag on the floor, I raced across the kitchen, turned off the flame, and shifted the pot to a different burner. A few angry drops of bubbling liquid leaped from the pot, spattering my hand. I yanked my hand back, hissing as the searing droplets touched my skin.

"Katya?"

I glanced up as Nina entered the room. A frown creased her forehead as her eyes locked on the specks of red I was now wiping off my hands with a dishcloth. An open book was, as usual, resting in her hands.

"The sauce—I'm so sorry!" she said frantically, eyes widening as she realized that her forgotten concoction had just attacked me. Judging by the way she was currently gaping at the pot, she was stunned by her neglect of the sauce. But I was no longer surprised by such scenarios— they were simply a part of living with her. After all, it was a known fact that whenever Nina picked up a book, she was automatically engrossed in it, and all other matters fled from her mind.

"It's alright," I replied. "I always wondered what it would be like to be pasta."

A breathy chuckle escaped Nina's lips. Yet she continued to hover nervously in the doorway.

"So, which book is it?" I asked conversationally, nodding at the volume clutched in her hands. Her eyes lit up at the question, and all uncertainty vanished from her features.

"*Pride and Prejudice*," she answered, prancing into the room and sliding into one of the chairs at the table. Then, just as I knew she would, she launched into an enthusiastic tirade about what she had read so far, her hands animatedly flying through the air and her voice increasing in speed and octave as she brought the story to life.

I listened half-heartedly, trying my hardest to give her my full attention—but my mind invariably wandered back to my strange meeting with Matteo. Staring at the hand that I had just finished freeing of tomato sauce—the same hand that Matteo had held so carefully in his own—I reflected on the feelings and sensations that had overpowered me when we touched.

What had caused it? Did other people ever experience something similar when meeting a new person? I certainly never had. So why did it happen this time?

And what about Matteo? Had he felt something similar?

Or was it time for me to start questioning my sanity?

"Kat? Are you alright?"

I looked up at Nina, who was gazing worriedly at me.

"What? Oh, yeah, I'm fine," I answered distractedly. "Why?"

"I was talking to you, but you weren't listening. You—"She paused. "What is the term? Ah, 'zoned out.'"

"Sorry," I murmured, flushing in guilt.

"You don't need to apologize," she replied in a kind voice. "I just wanted to make sure you're okay. I'm sorry if I was rambling."

"No, no, it's not you," I assured her. "I just have a lot on my mind. Something happened today that was kind of... weird."

"What do you mean?"

"I don't know how to explain it," I sighed. Then, quieter, I added, "You'll think I'm crazy if I tell you."

"You know I won't," she stated firmly. I stared at her

for a long moment, biting my lip. Nina was right. I knew she wouldn't judge me for anything I told her. She was the one person in the world who never had. It was one of the things I loved most about her—the rare gift she had for remaining open-minded and compassionate no matter what.

"I met a guy on my way home," I began, making my way over to the table and sinking into the chair across from her. "Well, actually, I kind of ran into him. Literally. I knocked him over and everything. His name is Matteo.

"It was odd, Nina. You know how socially awkward I am. I don't *do* conversation. I'm bad at it. But with him..." I paused, a small smile tugging at my lips. "I don't know. It was easy. Comfortable. We had a really nice talk. I even told him about my family. Not everything, just... the basics."

"That doesn't sound too weird to me. Unusual for you, yes; but not weird."

"Oh, don't worry, there's more," I promised. "You see, when we introduced ourselves to each other—" I paused, unsure how to give voice to everything I had experienced.

"Kat, what happened?" Nina probed gently. My eyes flickered to hers, and I felt somewhat reassured by the patience that shimmered in the green depths.

"What I'm about to tell you is going to sound totally insane, like something from a romantic comedy," I said, trying to reassure both Nina and myself of my soundness of mind. After all, I was a historian—I dealt with facts. But what I experienced today? It was straight from fiction. I knew how ridiculous it was all going to sound.

"You know how I feel about things like fate and romance," I continued with a bit more cynicism than I intended. "I don't believe in any of it. I *can't*—especially considering what I am."

Nina nodded silently in understanding, her eyes filling with sympathy. This time, it wasn't my identity as a historian that I was talking about, and she knew it. I took a deep breath.

"When Matteo and I touched, a warmth spread throughout my body. I'm not being metaphorical here," I clarified. "I literally felt warmer inside. It was like..." I paused, seeking the right words. "Sunlight seeping through my veins, into my heart and soul.

"Then, everything around us seemed to fade away— the people, the buildings. Even time itself disappeared." I closed my eyes, my voice growing tender as the memory flooded my mind. "It felt like Matteo was the only thing still anchoring me to the Earth's surface. Nothing else existed or mattered. In that moment, he was my entire world, and everything began and ended with *him*.

"It was like we had become one. I could see all of his emotions in his eyes—they're so expressive. It was like looking into his soul," I breathed, the words now flowing from my mouth like the water of a steady river. "And I could *feel* them, Nina. Somehow, inside of me, I could feel his emotions."

"Wow," Nina whispered reverently, watching me with an awestruck expression. "It's like something from a story."

"Nina—" I began warily. She quickly raised a hand to silence me.

"I know, I know—you don't believe in romance." She punctuated her words with an eye roll, then leaned forward, resting her elbows against the table. "But all stories, even the most imaginative ones, usually have some degree of truth in real life."

She allowed her words to sink in for a moment before adding, "What you just described to me—I've heard it described by other people before."

"You have?" I asked eagerly. "Do you know what it was?"

"I do, but you're not going to like it," she informed me with an apologetic tone. I swallowed nervously.

"Just tell me," I insisted weakly.

"I don't think I have to." She directed a pointed look at my left hand, where it was resting on the table. Her jade eyes were sparkling with wonder, and a radiant smile played on her lips. Following her gaze, I glanced down. Spotting some strange discoloration peeking out from beneath the cuff of my sweater, I hurriedly rolled up my sleeve. Then, I gasped. Encircling my wrist, as though tattooed on my skin, was a design—a braid consisting of two strands, one blue and one red. It was simple, yet intricate. Beautiful, yet intimidating. Comforting, yet terrifying.

I knew without a doubt that it hadn't been there this morning. And I had a feeling that I knew exactly when it had appeared.

"How?" I breathed, running my fingers reverently over the mark. A familiar warmth tingled across my skin as I traced the entwined bands of blue and red. For some reason, that was what finally made me register that the mark was real.

And then the panic struck.

"Nina, what is this?" I squeaked.

"A soulmark, if my guess is correct," she replied easily,

as though it were the most obvious thing in the world.

"No—no, it isn't. It can't be," I spluttered in denial, rubbing in vain at the red and blue strands in an attempt to rid myself of them.

"It is, Kat," she affirmed gently.

"But it can't be!" I flew from my chair, pacing around the kitchen like a caged animal. "I know what this is—it's a dream. This whole day has been a dream, so none of it is actually happening. It's not real."

"Kat—"

"Ok, maybe all of this *is* real. But this isn't a soulmark," I asserted, pointing at my wrist. "It's a tattoo. Yes—that's it! Someone must have gotten me drunk while I was doing research in the library today. I must have gotten this tattoo while under the influence."

"Kat—"

"No, no, that doesn't make sense. I haven't had anything to drink today. So, maybe it's not alcohol." I continued to pace, muttering to myself. "Aha! Artistic fairies! That must be it. They kidnapped me and—"

"KAT!"

I froze, gazing wide-eyed at Nina.

"Do you even hear yourself?" she asked incredulously. "Artistic fairies? Really?" She sighed. "Look, I know this is a lot for you to take in, and I understand why. But you need to face the facts. That," she pointed at my wrist "is a soulmark."

"But I wasn't born with it. Vaettir are always born with a soulmark, unless the Norns choose not to give them a soulmate. You can't just... *get* a soulmark magically one day. That doesn't happen."

"I know," Nina nodded calmly. "But there are always

exceptions to every rule."

"But I'm a Daski," I protested. "Daskis never have soulmates. It's the curse the Norns bestowed upon us as punishment for being a breed of monsters."

"Not all of you are monsters, Kat," Nina argued.

"Nina—" I countered unhappily.

"Alright, alright," Nina conceded, raising her hands in surrender. "That's not the point, right now anyway." She rested her elbows on the table, cradling her chin in her hands. "But Kat, you can't deny the facts. You have a mark that for all intents and purposes has a lot of striking similarities to a soulmark." She held up her right hand, revealing her own soulmark—a solid band of ombre blues and greens on her ring finger. "You didn't have that mark this morning. Between then and now, the only notable thing that happened to you was that you met Matteo. And from what you described of your encounter with him, it sounds almost identical to tunnistaa, soulbond recognition.

"According to all of the things I've heard from other people, soulbonds are dormant until two soulmates meet for the first time. When that happens, their souls go through a process of identifying each other as their other half, which ignites the bond. Apparently, it's a remarkable experience—completely life-altering. My nonna once told me that, when she met my nonno, it was like finding a piece of herself she hadn't known was missing." A dreamy look entered Nina's eyes. "Suddenly, her entire life made sense.

"It sounds exactly like what happened between you and Matteo. Of course, I'm just speculating here. I can't be one hundred percent sure. But everything adds up to him being your soulmate."

Silence fell over the kitchen. Only the loud ticking of the clock above the sink interrupted the stillness. I gaped at Nina, my mouth opening and closing several times like a fish gasping for air. My body felt numb, paralyzed with shock. Even my mind, which was usually whirring with endless activity, was blank, as though my brain had completely short-circuited.

Nina waited patiently as I struggled to collect myself, observing the minute shifts in my features as the information seeped into my consciousness and, after a few minutes, finally started to be processed by my sluggish mind.

"He's my soulmate," I croaked once I regained the ability to speak.

"Most likely," Nina commented cheerfully.

"But... how?" My hand subconsciously drifted to the pale blue necklace that I always wore, my fingers fidgeting with the beads. For fifteen years, the kedja had concealed my identity as a Daski from the world, hiding it from humans and Vaettirs alike. It locked my powers away, preventing me from using them. Without it, I was a danger to everyone around me. The ice flowing through my veins had the ability to both injure and kill. Even with my iron control over my magic, it was still far too volatile to be allowed any freedom. The slightest slip in concentration or the smallest flood of emotion could spell disaster for those near me.

So, I kept the thin strand of beads on at all times. It protected the world from me, and gave me some semblance of a normal life. I could go out, talk to people, have friends. All without fear that I might accidentally kill them. All without fear that they might discover that I was, by nature, a monster—born into the most despised race of Vaettir. It was a race of criminals and murderers, whose hearts had been turned cold by the ice within them.

Nina knew the truth about me, of course. We had been best friends for almost a decade. We were practically sisters. Besides, Nina was different from most other people. She saw beyond my identity as a Daski. She understood me.

A soulmate was a much more complicated matter. How could I possibly hide my ancestry from someone bound to me in the most intimate way possible? How could I protect them from myself forever?

"I shouldn't have a soulmate," I uttered miserably. Then, still unable to explain this new development, I repeated, "Daskis don't get soulmates."

"True. But you're not like most Daskis. You're an exception to the rule—always have been. So, maybe you're an exception with this, too."

"But why me? Why would *I*, of all people, be different?"

Nina didn't respond, but gave me a sympathetic look. I sighed, crossing the kitchen and sinking tiredly back into my seat at the table.

"What do I do now?"

"I think you should talk to Matteo again. If my theory is right, then he's a Vaettir, too. He has to be, since we're the only beings that the Norns gifted with soulmates. So, see if his soulmark matches yours. If it does, then he's your soulmate, and what you experienced today really was tunnistaa."

"What if he *is* my soulmate?" I asked hesitantly.

"Then we'll find a way to make it work between the two of you."

"And if he's not?"

"Then you're just weird," she shrugged, giving me a playful smirk. I huffed in feigned offense, throwing the sauce-stained dishcloth at her. She squawked as the towel hit her, a string of giggles escaping her lips.

"Matteo asked me to go to the San Nicolò celebrations with him tomorrow," I confessed, watching distractedly as Nina lifted the dishcloth from her lap and discarded it on the table in front of her.

"He did?" She quirked an eyebrow. "What did you say?"

"I said I would."

"Excellent!" she exclaimed, clapping her hands together. "Then you'll need an outfit. And I have just the thing."

Before I could respond, Nina was already across the kitchen and vanishing down the hall. As I listened to her light footsteps retreating towards her room—presumably to find whatever clothing she had decided I was going to wear tomorrow—I shook my head fondly. As much as I admired Nina's optimism, as much as I wanted her to be right about this, as much as I wanted to believe in a happy ending as much as she did... I couldn't let myself hope. Not yet. Maybe not ever.

After all, I was a Daski by birth. And no Daski had ever escaped the scourge of seclusion. In the end, either our powers or the curse of the Norns saw to it that we forever lived our lives alone.

CHAPTER THREE

"No."

"Kat—"

"Absolutely not."

"But Kat—"

"It has frills!"

"They're cute!"

"I'm not wearing anything that can be classified as cute."

"What about elegant?"

"Nina—"

"Fine." She rummaged through the closet one more time, pulling out a navy dress. "What about this one, then?"

I eyed it skeptically, which earned an exasperated sigh from Nina.

"Come on, Kat. You didn't like the frilly one, you didn't like the pink one—"

"Because it was pink!" I exclaimed in horror.

"Well, this one isn't frilly or pink." She held it up higher, examining it. "Besides, the color would bring out your eyes."

My jaw clenched. Why Nina was forcing me to wear a dress for my meeting—Nina insisted it was a date—with Matteo was beyond me. It wasn't like we were going to a gala. We were going to be hanging out in Campo Santo Stefano. At night. In winter. It was hardly necessary to wear a dress, and probably somewhat impractical.

Though, if you asked me, dresses were generally impractical regardless of the situation. One miscalculation in retrieving a fallen object, one moment of ill-positioning while sitting, one misdirected gust of wind, could spell the difference between classiness and humiliation.

It was one of the reasons I hated wearing dresses. Though, I wasn't fond of the vulnerability they instilled within me, either.

Yet here I was, forced against my will to choose a dress that I had to wear to the Festa di San Nicolò. And of the three options with which Nina provided me, I knew which one was the least objectionable...

Which is how I ended up wearing the simple, navy blue dress that was currently hugging my body. I dubiously eyed the fabric flowing around my legs. I might not have been happy about it, but at least it was my favorite color. It also didn't have frills, or glitter, or anything else that Nina thought would look "festive."

Plus, in a happy twist of fate, today was much warmer than yesterday, and entirely devoid of wind—which meant that I was neither freezing, nor in fear of pulling a Marilyn Monroe. That, in itself, was a relief. Apparently, Mother Nature recognized that I had enough to worry about, and had decided to take pity on me.

Speaking of things to worry about...

My fingers fidgeted unconsciously with the sleeve of my jacket, tugging it down further over the soulmark beneath it. A soulmark I wasn't supposed to have.

I sighed. I hated being a Daski. It was like constantly fighting a losing battle—in everything.

True, I wasn't a thief or murderer like most Daskis. But because of my nature, I would forever be labelled as one. I would also always be more disposed to become one. That was the trouble with being half frost jotun.

Of course, like all Vaettir, I was also half human. But human genetics didn't matter much for any of the Vaettir, outside of making us mortal and giving us a human appearance. The only thing that truly made a difference in Vaettir society was magical heritage.

For the Daskis, all of the odds were against us. Frost jotuns were hated by the Vanir and Aesir alike, and for good reason. They were evil. It was as plain and simple as that. As such, any Vaettir with frost jotun blood—in other words, Daskis—were considered to be scum across all the realms. The only place we might have been accepted was Jotunheim, the home of the frost jotuns. But, even the frost jotuns hated Daskis because of their "contaminated" blood. Apparently, being half human didn't score any points on Jotunheim.

As though being considered socially unworthy wasn't bad enough, the Daskis were also perpetually hunted by the Voktere—the guardians of Earth. The Voktere were valued members of Vaettir society, descended from ancient elemental spirits who had mated with humans. They inherited the powers of their ancestors, using them to protect the people of Earth from the forces of evil. Unfortunately, those forces often included the Daskis. And although all of the Voktere were dedicated to monitoring the activities of known Daskis, no group was more infamous for their treatment of Daskis than the Salamanders.

Descended from spirits of fire, Salamanders had the power to create, control, and manipulate the element at will. They were known to be warm people with fiery personalities. Yet they also possessed hot tempers and a passionate abhorrence for Daskis. They took it upon themselves to track down any Daskis they could, hunting them like animals, slaughtering them. It was said that many Salamanders liked to use fire to torture the "ice monsters" they captured, holding them for months in hellish imprisonment before finally killing them.

As a Daski, I was raised to fear Salamanders more than any other living creature in the universe. I could still recall with perfect clarity the stories my parents used to tell me about the unfortunate Daskis who had been caught by Salamanders; the demands that I learn to control my powers at all costs, lest I be discovered as a Daski. To this day, the thought of encountering a Salamander terrified me.

Thankfully, fate had been on my side the day I met Nina. She wasn't Salamander, but rather an Undine—a water elemental. Like the epitome of the traditional Undine, she was calm, compassionate, and easy-going. At times, perhaps a bit too much.

Then, there were the Sylphs and Gnomes. Sylphs not only controlled the wind—they *were* the wind. Whimsical, flighty, gentle, but scarily powerful when angered, they were the rarest of all the Voktere. Gnomes, on the other hand, were the most common. They were firm and dependable, just like the earth they manipulated. They also tended to be stubborn and unbending, which frequently put them at odds with the more flexible Undines.

I was jealous of the Voktere. Although all Vaettir lived in secret among humans, the Voktere had infinitely more freedom than the Daskis. For starters, they weren't hated by the entire universe. Quite the opposite. They were entrusted by the deities with protecting the human race, and were thus honored as great warriors. There was no need for them to hide the way Daskis did. Moreover, they could enter into platonic and romantic relationships with any other Voktere. There was no risk involved, no threat of injury or death. Their powers were much calmer, much more controlled, than those of the Daskis.

It seemed that the only thing they couldn't do was marry a Kongelig. The elite of Vaettir society, Kongeligs were descended from the gods and goddesses themselves. They were the rarest breed of Vaettir, and famous for three things: their competency as archers, their incomparable fearlessness, and their uncanny powers of perception. Of the two types of Kongeligs—Ullr and Vali—the latter were the most beloved. They had warm, gentle, bright personalities that meshed perfectly with their control over sunlight.

Ullr, who, like Daskis, manipulated ice, received a much more negative reception in Vaettir communities. The Ullr were reputed to be cruel, brutal, tyrannical. They were feared by all the Vaettir. Only their devotion to justice and their blood connections to the Vanir and Aesir prevented them from being viewed with the same loathing as the Daskis.

It was frustrating that something as uncontrollable as lineage could mean the difference between being honored or condemned by society.

A light breeze gusted through the campo, and I shivered, silently cursing Nina for making me wear this stupid dress. Pulling my jacket tighter around myself, my thoughts drifted to Matteo. Nina was right—if he really was my soulmate, then he also had to be a Vaettir. He wasn't a Daski. Of that, I was certain. And I doubted that he was a Kongelig. Which meant that he was a Voktere. But which one? He seemed reliable and strong, so perhaps he was a Gnome. Although he was also extremely gentle, and had been nothing but calm after I ran into him. So, perhaps an Undine then.

How was I supposed to find out for sure? Should I ask him outright, or infer it from his personality? Was it better to figure it out before I told him about the mark on my wrist, or after? And speaking of the mark... what if he didn't have one matching mine? Or, worse, what if he did? How was I supposed to tell him then that I was a Daski? What if he hated me for it? What if he rejected me, rejected our bond? Everything told me that he should. I was a member of an inferior race, not to mention a breed of known monsters.

But what if he didn't reject me? Things could end badly. We would have to hide for the rest of our lives. He would constantly be at risk of being outcast by Vaettir society. If he had a Vaettir boss, he could lose his job.

Without a doubt, he would lose his status as a Voktere, and be forever labeled a traitor to his race. It could cost him his family, his friends.

And, given the volatility of my nature, possibly even his life.

"Katya?" The familiar voice snapped me out of my thoughts. Matteo was standing in front of me. Dark jeans and a simple, yet striking emerald sweater adorned his thin, muscular body. Black, square-rimmed glasses—the same ones that had been jostled from his nose when I ran into him yesterday—framed his large, expressive eyes. Resting lightly on his lips was the trademark crooked smile that so easily made me forget how to breathe.

Silhouetted by the golden glow of the sun, he was nearly ethereal in appearance.

"Ciao Matteo," I greeted, impressed by how strong my voice sounded in spite of the skipping of my heart. Apparently, it didn't take much to turn me into a blushing teenager again.

"You look nice."

"Grazie," I mumbled shyly, tucking a stray strand of hair behind my ear. "You look nice, too." Which, of course, was an understatement. He was breathtaking—and he was made even more so by the faint pink that endearingly tinged his cheeks as he murmured his thanks.

"So, I was thinking..." he began, clearing his throat. "Maybe we could watch the canal procession, and then grab dinner on Torcello?"

"That sounds wonderful," I answered brightly. He beamed, his smile as bright as the sun.

"Terrific. Shall we?" He extended his elbow, and I giggled—oh, god, now I was *giggling*?—at the gesture.

Slipping my hand over his arm, we set off across the campo toward the grand canal.

Murano's boat parade was the highlight of the Festa di San Nicolò every year. Transitioning the festival from its public daytime activities to its more personal nighttime celebrations, the procession was always a joyous and lively event. This year was no different.

Matteo and I stood beside the canal, our toes brushing its edge, as the floating parade began. One by one, the boats drifted along—gondolas, vaporetti, dinghies. Each was packed with people waving colorful streamers and singing traditional songs. Spectators along the canal waved at the water-borne travelers. Some chatted amicably with their friends and neighbors, others joined in with the melodies drifting to them from the passing vessels. Among them, young children sprinted back and forth. They weaved in and out, laughing in glee as they chased each other through the onlookers.

In this jovial atmosphere, it was easy to forget about the doubts and fears that had been plaguing me for the past twenty-four hours. And forget I did.

It wasn't until after we had finished dinner that I was inadvertently reminded of it all.

Matteo and I were strolling along the main canal of Torcello. Beside us, the water swished gently, its movements aligned with the ebb and flow of the distant Adriatic. Reflected on its rippling surface were the countless twinkling stars that filled the inky night sky.

We passed an elderly couple who was out enjoying a moonlit promenade. They nodded politely in greeting, then continued on their way. Other than that, the canal path was empty. All other living souls on this nearly deserted island were either asleep or still at the restaurant we had just left. The occasional lilting laughter of the latter was the only reminder of their presence.

I sighed in contentment. Wandering arm in arm with Matteo in a world blanketed by the pale glow of the moon, the soft notes of "Al Di La" drifting to us from the osteria, I felt full in more ways than one.

On the one hand, my stomach was satisfied from the meal of pasta and wine that Matteo and I had shared. More importantly, though, my heart was positively bursting with happiness. Never in my wildest dreams had I ever expected to meet someone who could make me feel the way Matteo did. Relationships with people—whether platonic or otherwise—were difficult for me. It always felt like everyone was expecting me to meld myself to their preconceived mold of who I should be—smarter, dumber, prettier, uglier, funnier, more outgoing, quieter. Who I was never seemed to be enough, never seemed to be accepted. Especially if you were my family, who just wanted me to *not* be the monster I was born to be.

But with Matteo, the opposite was true. It was easy to be myself around him.

When I rambled about stories from history that anyone else would find boring... he listened intently, watching me with something akin to fondness.

When I made a joke that no one else would understand because of my somewhat dry sense of humor... he laughed, the sound genuine and rich with sincerity.

When I could only nod in response to his stories, uncertain of how to respond due to my lack of social finesse... he didn't interpret it as a lack of interest. Instead, he continued talking and laughing with me as though I were the most extraordinary conversationalist he'd ever met.

The way he acted around me, the way he treated me... it was like the perfect blend of yin and yang. He had a gift for story-telling and banter, yet he remained riveted by everything I said like I possessed a silver tongue. He waited with patience each time I stumbled over my words, never interrupting, never judging or mocking my mouth's inability to keep up with my mind.

He was funny, but he understood when a degree of seriousness was required. He was talented, but humble. He was intelligent, but not pedantic. He was honest, but never cruel. He was chivalrous, but never chauvinistic.

He was a bright light of everything that was good in the world. Yet he didn't have the artificial glare of a spotlight. Rather, he was the sun—real and genuine, warm and gentle; retaining a natural ability for illumination, but always willing to surrender his own prominence so that other celestial objects and elements of nature could showcase their aptitudes as well.

Being with Matteo was effortless and comfortable. It just felt *right* in a way that nothing else in my life ever had. And it filled my heart and soul with a tranquility, a serenity, a peaceful contentment that swelled in my core.

"What happened with your family?"

"What?" I asked, caught off-guard by the quiet question.

"Yesterday, you mentioned that you had a strained relationship with your family. What happened?"

"Oh, uh—" I hesitated, biting my lip. There it was—the single inquiry, deceptively simple in appearance, that would force me to reveal *everything* to Matteo.

Was that something I was prepared to do? Could I really bring myself to risk this fragile connection we had by revealing the truth about my family, my past, my very identity?

Sure, I was comfortable being around him. That wasn't the issue.

The problem was that I was falling for him. Even after only knowing him one day, I already felt an inexplicable desire to be closer to him—the subtle tugging of our bonds as they yearned for us to be closer.

Selfishly, I wasn't ready to lose him. I probably never would be. But, eventually, he'd find out the truth. He'd discover that we were too different to be together. We were opposites—he was summer, I was winter; he was warmth, I was coldness; he was light, I was darkness. It could never work.

And once Matteo knew what I was, once he realized that our soulbond was an impossibility, he would disappear in the blink of an eye. Whether his departure from my life would be a result of disgust or practicality, it didn't matter. All that did matter was that, one way or another, Matteo would leave. There would be no reason for him to stay. It would be insanity if he did.

So, why was there a part of me that hoped he would? Why was there a part of me that wished for him to learn of what I was and still accept me despite it? Why did I dream of him taking my hand, pledging his undying love to me, gazing deep into my eyes as he promised to fight to keep me? Why did I hope that, somehow, we could defy the odds to be together?

I was pulled from my tumultuous thoughts by a hand gently tugging me to a stop. I looked over at Matteo in confusion as my mind quieted and the stillness of Torcello engulfed me once more.

"I'm sorry if I crossed a line," he said tenderly. "You don't have to answer if you don't want to."

"No, no, it's fine," I assured him. Glancing down at the hand that was covering my own, the light strands of blue and red around my wrist peeked out from beneath the cuff of my jacket. "I just—"

Don't want you to hate me.

Don't want to lose you before I even get to know you.

Don't want you to see me as a monster the way the rest of our world does—the way I do.

"—don't know where to begin," I finished.

"I've always found the beginning to be a good place." He gave my hand a soft squeeze of encouragement. A familiar warmth tingled through my hand, up my arm, and spread through my body. Immediately, my fear vanished, replaced instead by an all-encompassing calm.

"You know you can tell me anything, right? After all, we're soulmates." He tapped a finger on my soulmark.

"You know about that?"

"Of course. I've had my mark since I was born." He pulled his own sleeve up just enough to reveal the same red and blue braid around his left wrist. "I had a feeling you were my soulmate after we met yesterday, but I wasn't sure until I caught a glimpse of your mark at dinner tonight."

"Oh. Um—are you mad?"

"Why, in all the realms, would I be mad?"

"I—"

Suddenly, there was a loud roar, cutting off my words before they even had a chance to leave my mouth. Flames erupted on the bridge just ahead of us, and I stumbled back a few steps, throwing up an arm to shield my eyes from the brightness of the flare. A wave of heat rippled across the brick pathway. The rancid odor of rotting meat assaulted my nose.

As the initial glare dwindled, I lowered my arm, my eyes seeking the source of the explosion. As soon as they did, a cold chill slithered through me.

In the middle of the stone bridge, standing tall against a background of spinning flames, was a figure. It had the form of a man, but there the similarities ended. Leathery gray skin the color of ash was stretched taught across the creature's face. Beneath two black horns, a pair of red eyes, like burning embers, gazed maliciously out at the world. A black cloak enveloped the creature's body, and an onyx pitchfork was clutched in one of its claw-like hands, the pointed tips glowing like molten metal.

From somewhere nearby, shutters squealed and doorknobs rattled as the sparse inhabitants of Torcello peered out at the ruckus. A chorus of curious voices floated along with the tide of people approaching from the osteria. From all corners of the island, people slowly began to converge on the area, the rumble of the creature's arrival being both deafening and unearthly. There were nervous whispers, intrigued pointing, slightly inebriated chuckles—until the beast rapped its pitchfork against the bricks beneath its feet.

"People of Venice," it boomed. The raspy, cold voice seemed to echo across the entire island. Matteo shifted closer to me, his hand clenching protectively around mine.

"More than two centuries ago, you signed a contract with me. Without any hesitation or deceit, I fulfilled my end of the bargain," the creature stated with feigned munificence. "You, however, did not. Still, I waited and waited. As is customary of my endless generosity, I gave you *countless* opportunities to satisfy the terms of your agreement. But for two hundred years now, you have cheated me out of my rightful payment. Now, the bill has come due."

At that moment, the swirling flames behind the creature flared to life, and two lines of cloaked figures emerged. They floated like specters down the steps, encircling the crowd that had gathered at the base of the bridge. A few people, having recognized the ominous gravity of the situation, tried to retreat from the scene.

As soon as they moved though, a ring of fire erupted from the ground, trapping everyone inside its blazing perimeter. Whips of fire snaked from the bony claws of the cloaked entities, cracking through the air as they herded everyone into a huddled, trembling mass. Shrieks of terror rent the air as people flinched away from the lashing flames, and fearful whimpers rippled through the assembled throng of Venetians.

"Consider tonight a demonstration of my generosity," the creature on the bridge hissed, baring its sharp, pointed teeth in a vicious smile. It gestured around at the circle of cloaked wraiths. "I could have destroyed you here and now. Instead, I come with a warning—and I offer you the chance to redeem yourselves."

"You have until the end of the day on the twenty-fourth of this month to deliver to me seven young souls of your choosing. If by the stroke of midnight, you have once again failed to honor your end of the contract, then I shall take any seven souls that I desire and lay waste to your precious city."

With another thump of the pitchfork against the brick bridge, the cloaked figures glided back up the steps and into the portal. When the last of them had disappeared, the horned creature cast one final glare across the cowering group of onlookers.

"This is your final chance," it threatened menacingly, before it, too, vanished into the flames. With a sizzle and a flourish of sparks, the circle of fire snapped closed, and the ring of flames surrounding us dispersed.

An eerie silence descended over the island, the world once again illuminated only by the pale glow of the moon. No one dared move for several long minutes. It was as though the entire population of Torcello was collectively holding its breath.

Eventually, though, a few brave individuals began to disperse. When it seemed that they were able to leave without any harm befalling them, others rushed away as well, desperate to flee the site of horror. Soon, there was only a handful of us remaining.

"What the hell was that?" gasped Matteo, snapping out of his state of shock. I shook my head, unable to speak. My mind was too busy sifting through the research I had been doing these past few months. The beast had mentioned a contract. Young souls. Something about it seemed familiar. Hadn't I read something similar in a book on Venetian legends recently? It was right there in my memory, drifting just out of reach—

Oh no.

"I think you just answered your own question."

"What do you mean?" he inquired, giving me a quizzical look. I didn't answer, having barely even registered that he had just asked me a question. Staring at the bridge a moment longer, I swallowed hard against the dread coursing through me.

"Come on," I said suddenly, grabbing his hand and pulling him toward the waiting vaporetto at the far end of the canal. "Let's go."

We hurried to the vessel, jostling our way on board alongside dozens of other people fleeing the island. The nervous energy on the boat was palpable. Fortunately, within a couple of minutes, we were out of the canal and into the Adriatic, heading back in the direction of Murano. As distance was placed between Torcello and the vaporetto, the other passengers calmed slightly, their anxious chatter turning into more relaxed conversation.

Still, I kept my eyes fixed on the dark outline of the bridge. I watched it growing smaller and smaller, trepidation gnawing at my gut, until it became one with the thick darkness surrounding it. If my theory about everything that had just happened was correct, then the people of Venice were in more trouble than they could even imagine.

CHAPTER FOUR

The moment I swung open the door to the apartment, Nina barreled into the kitchen.

"Kat! You're back! How was—" She froze as she took in my frazzled expression. Her look of concern quickly morphed into one of confusion as Matteo awkwardly shuffled into the room behind me.

"Nina, this is Matteo," I informed distractedly, gesturing toward him with a wave of my hand before moving in the direction of the den.

"Ciao," Matteo greeted, his tone tense and uncertain— as though he was afraid of Nina's reaction to his surprise appearance in her home.

Entering the living area of our apartment, I didn't hear Nina's response. My mind was too preoccupied with my current mission. I made a beeline for the bookshelf that we kept in the corner. It was ancient—a relic that had been left here by a previous owner. Between Nina and myself, it had quickly become crammed with tomes of all ages, colors, and sizes. Truth be told, we probably asked too much of the warped oak shelves, considering the way they groaned in protest each time we added another book to the collection.

I ran my finger along the spines of the various volumes, seeking the one book for which I was searching. It was hardly an easy task. There were classic novels, nonfiction works about history, informational texts on Vaettir, cookbooks, used textbooks from our college years, an electrician's manual for who knows what reason—aha! My forefinger paused on the edge of a particularly large book, its old leather cover dry and cracking with age.

Carefully sliding it from its designated spot, I carried it back into the kitchen.

"What happened?" I heard Nina ask as I stepped through the doorway.

"There was an attack," Matteo replied.

"An attack?" Nina's voice rose with incredulity. "By who? And why?"

"I don't know."

"I think I do," I cut in.

Setting the book on the table with a loud *thump*, I slid into a chair and started flipping through the pages, only stopping once I found the chapter I was looking for. Across the top of the page, scrawled in thick gothic font, were the words "Il Ponte del Diavolo."

"The Devil's Bridge?" Nina slipped into the chair beside me, confusion furrowing her brow.

"You know how the research I've been doing hasn't

been adding up?"

Nina nodded silently.

"Well, I think that's because I've been looking at Venetian folklore as precisely that—a series of legends. But what if they're not legends? What if the reason nothing makes sense about it all is because they're *actually* tales of Venice's history."

"Huh?"

"What Matteo and I saw on Torcello tonight is remarkably similar to this legend," I said, pointing at the black words arcing across the page. "A little over two centuries ago, Venice was invaded by Austria. Throughout the occupation, the city was inhabited by Austrian soldiers. During his time in Venice, one of those soldiers fell in love with a Venetian woman—and she with him. Their romance flourished, and soon they wanted to be married.

"Unfortunately, given the circumstances of the soldier's presence in Venice, the woman's family disapproved of the union. Despite this, the soldier and the woman continued to see each other secretly. They even planned to run off together. But on the night they were to elope, the soldier was captured by the woman's father and neighbors. They killed him."

"That's horrible," Nina sighed despondently.

"The woman was heartbroken. In her distress, she called upon a witch who lived just outside of the city limits, hoping that the sorceress would be able to revive the dead soldier. But the witch's magic couldn't bring someone back from the dead. Wanting to help the distraught woman, the witch turned to a being that she knew possessed the power of resurrection—the Devil.

"So, the young woman went to the nearest bridge—" I

pointed at the small illustration at the corner of the page, which depicted a small, brick bridge that bore a striking resemblance to the one that had been the site of our own terrifying encounter earlier that evening.

"The bridge we were at tonight," Matteo breathed in recognition. I nodded, continuing.

"—and walked over it three times with a lit candle. By doing so, she summoned the Devil."

"The witch mediated a contract between the two, with the Devil agreeing to resuscitate the executed soldier. With the witch as a witness, both the woman and the Devil signed the contract—the woman with her own blood, the Devil with the fires of Hell. True to his word, the Devil used the Key of Time to bring the soldier back to life. Overjoyed by their reunion, the woman and the soldier ran off together. They were never seen again."

"What about the Devil?" Nina asked. "I mean, yes, he kept his promise to revive the soldier, but... he's the Devil. I highly doubt that he made the gesture out of the goodness of his heart. So, what was in it for him? What did the woman promise him in return for her fiancé's return?"

"The souls of seven children," I answered solemnly. "The witch was supposed to deliver seven of Venice's children to the Devil the next day—December twenty-fourth."

I glanced over at Matteo, the words "twenty-fourth" silently forming on his lips as he made the connection.

"Supposed to?" Nina probed.

"The witch chose seven children, rounded them up, and was on her way back to the bridge to give them to the Devil. But she was killed before they reached their destination. The kids ran back to their homes, and the Devil was left waiting in perpetuity for the witch." I turned the page in the book, only to be met with a sketch of a familiar gray-skinned, horned creature with glowing red eyes.

"Now, according to the legend, the Devil returns to the bridge every year on the twenty-fourth of December to collect payment of the souls of the seven children."

A heavy silence fell over the kitchen like a thick blanket. Nina was staring at the book on the table, her face panicked. Matteo, on the other hand, appeared to be stuck somewhere between disbelief and shock.

"Wait, so you're saying that the creature we saw on Torcello... was the Devil?"

"Yes."

A moment passed, then another. And then Nina exploded in denial.

"But it couldn't have been! According to the legend, the Devil only appears on Torcello once a year—on December twenty-fourth. Today is only the sixth."

She had a point. It seemed that the Devil only ever made annual visits to the small island on Christmas Eve. Which begged the question of how—and why—he had shown up three weeks early.

"What if someone summoned him?"

Both Nina and I turned our attention to Matteo, who had a thoughtful expression on his face.

"What do you mean?" Nina questioned with dread in her voice.

"Well, there was no record of the Devil ever being seen in Torcello until he was summoned there by the woman in the legend. After that, he only appeared on the day he was supposed to collect the children's souls. It's like that's the *only* day he was permitted to return to Torcello, since he was legitimately owed a payment," Matteo explained as he took the seat across from me. "So, it would make sense that if he's suddenly breaking the pattern and showing up on different days, then it's because someone summoned him here."

"Who would do that?" Nina sounded rather faint, sagging against the table.

"It could be anyone," I answered. "Someone who worships the Devil, a kid pulling a prank or fulfilling a dare, someone desperate for help like the woman from the legend..."

"Well that narrows it down," she muttered unhappily.

"What about the cloaked figures we saw?" Matteo asked.

"Cloaked figures?"

"The Devil showed up with an army of these tall, thin, cloaked creatures," I clarified for Nina, who looked equally baffled and horrified. "They had whips of fire, and could use the element for just about anything, judging by the way flames were sprouting up everywhere."

"Whips of fire?" she squeaked as I started flipping through the book again. "*Whips of fire?!*"

I felt bad. Nina was definitely struggling to process all of this. For someone who was so passionate about stories—especially ones involving magic and myths—Nina much preferred for any adventures she was a part of to remain on paper. The fact that a horror story was now playing out in her real life, and now she was inadvertently being swept up into it? It was a bit too much for her to handle.

"There!" I exclaimed, stopping at an illustration midway through the book. Beneath the header reading "Gli Onemdi" was a drawing of a skeleton, a dark brown cloak draped over it, and a whip—the handle attached to a tail of flames—clutched in its bony fingers. "I knew they seemed familiar." I shivered inadvertently. It was rather disturbing to see one of those figures again, even if it was only an image in a book. "I would say that looks like what we saw tonight, wouldn't you?"

"Yeah, that's definitely it," Matteo confirmed.

"What is it now?" Nina groaned.

"Gli Onemdi—demons of the underworld," I replied, eyes scanning the text on the page. "In life, they were people who committed unspeakable crimes. When they died, they were sent to the Underworld and sentenced to an eternity under the Devil's command. They are his personal army, and must do whatever he bids of them. He furnished them with whips of fire, and granted them the ability to manipulate the element to their will."

"They can control fire," Matteo murmured. I glanced over at him. He was gazing at the page with an odd expression on his face. His lips were pressed into a thin line, and there was something deeply troubled in the pinched expression that had settled on his face.

"Oh, that's just great," Nina muttered sarcastically. "The Devil, evil dead people who are now the Devil's personal henchmen and have total control over the most dangerous element in the world... This couldn't get any worse."

"Well..." I started.

"Oh no," Nina shook her head. "Don't even tell me there's more. What else could there *possibly* be?"

"Just the fact that the Devil demanded payment of the

seven children by the twenty-fourth and vowed to destroy Venice if they're not delivered," I responded. Then, reluctantly, I added, "And it's up to us to make sure neither of those things happens."

It was so silent for a moment that you could've heard a pin drop. Then, Nina squeaked in alarm, "What do you mean, 'us?'"

"Well, there were very few of us on the island to begin with, so there aren't many people who even *know* about the Devil's ultimatum."

"That doesn't mean *we* have to do something about it.

"Yes, it does."

"No."

"Nina—"

"Nope."

"Nina, we're Vaettir. It's our responsibility to protect the people here from harm. We don't have a choice over the matter."

"Well, technically you do," she retorted bitterly.

"Yeah, and I choose to serve alongside you as a Voktere," I snapped.

"You're both Voktere, too?" Matteo asked.

"Well, she is." I jabbed a thumb in Nina's direction. "I'm—" I snapped my mouth shut, stopping myself before I could say any more. Then something else occurred to me. "Wait, what do you mean, 'too?'"

"I'm also a Voktere." Huh. Well, at least now I knew I had been right about that.

"So, it's up to the three of us to figure something out."

"Honestly, what can we even do about it?" Nina's gaze shifted between me and Matteo, her wide, fearful eyes practically begging us to reconsider. "We're three Vaettir.

He's *the Devil*. And apparently, he has an army of minions that could turn us all to ash if they wanted. I mean, seriously, Kat! I'm an Undine—a *water elemental*. Last time I checked, water and fire don't exactly mix. And you're—"

"Nina!" I cut her off sharply.

"Right, sorry." She coughed. "Look, long story short—nothing about us trying to fight the forces of Hell seems like a good idea."

"What other choice do we have? We can't sacrifice any children," I stated bluntly.

"Of course not," Nina agreed without hesitation. "But... well, are we sure he'll destroy Venice if the children aren't given to him?"

"We can't be sure of anything. But he said that if there weren't seven children waiting at that bridge for him by the stroke of midnight on December twenty-fourth, then he would take seven souls himself and then 'lay waste' to the city."

"So, what do we do?"

"I don't know," I murmured, staring at the book on the table as though willing it to give me an answer.

"Do you think there's an answer in the books you've been reading for your research?"

"As far as I know, I haven't come across anything that could help us," I admitted with a tired sigh. "But to be fair, at the time I was more focused on the folklore itself rather than potential ways to fight the Devil if he were to hypothetically appear in Venice. That's not exactly a contingency I thought I'd have to be prepared for." I shrugged. "We could always try taking another look though. At the very least, it couldn't hurt."

"I think that's a good idea," Matteo commented, breaking his silence. "I'll have my brother help us. The more people we have working on this, the faster we'll find a solution."

"Your brother won't mind?"

"Not at all. He loves adventures—even death-defying ones. This will be right up his alley."

"Okay," I said slowly, quirking a brow in vague curiosity and mild concern.

"Besides, he's a Voktere, too. It's his duty to protect Venice as much as it is ours," he added.

"Then it's settled. The four of us will head to the library tomorrow morning—"

"That's the only good thing about this situation," muttered Nina. I couldn't stop my snort of amusement. It would seem that even an impending fight with the Devil and his army of demons couldn't dampen her love of libraries.

"—and with a little luck, hopefully we'll be able to find *something* that will help us save Venice and everyone in it."

CHAPTER FIVE

Nina and I were seated at a corner table in the café where we had agreed to meet Matteo and his brother. As usual, Nina was reading. It was no longer *Pride and Prejudice*, I noted. Rather, *The Decameron* seemed to be Nina's new pursuit.

I stared into my cup of coffee, watching absently as white wisps of steam curled out of the murky liquid. Around us, the café was buzzing with early morning activity—quiet chatter, groggy orders, the clinking and whirring of various machines. Combined with the steady patter of the rain outside the window, it was almost soothing.

Yet my nerves were on edge. I wasn't sure why. It could have been residual apprehension from last night, the looming threat of Hell's wrath upon Venice. Maybe it was the knowledge that we were unlikely to find anything to help us solve Venice's dilemma given the sparse and often missing information in the books related to it. It could have been the general uncertainty that always came with meeting someone new. Or, perhaps it was the fact that I was seeing Matteo again.

I twirled that latter point around in my brain. In the chaos of the previous day, all thoughts of my soulbond with Matteo had been pushed to the back of my mind. The matters with which we were currently faced were inarguably more pressing.

Nevertheless, impatience gnawed at my insides. The longer I thought about the soulbond, the less terrifying it seemed. And the more time I spent with Matteo, the more I wanted to be tied to him for an eternity.

Of course, there was still a large part of me that feared our bond, too. It was still possible that Matteo would reject me once he discovered I was a Daski. It was also possible that I could seriously injure, even kill him, if my powers were ever unleashed.

But if Matteo could overlook what I was—and I was fairly certain, based on what I knew of him, that he would—and as long as I kept my powers locked away, then maybe, just maybe, it could work.

"Ciao Katya, Nina." I glanced up. As if on cue, there was Matteo, standing beside us. "Buongiorno."

"Vi presento il mio fratello, Emiliano," he said, gesturing to the man next to him.

"Leo," the latter amended. Taller than Matteo by several inches, Leo had an air of silent energy around him. His movements were quick and fluid, but possessed a franticness that spoke to a flighty spirit. Vivacity and curiosity sparkled in his honey eyes.

"Piacere," I said, taking his proffered hand.

"You must be Kat." He observed me for a moment, quirking his head. Then, before I even had time to register what was happening, he launched forward, wrapping his arms around me in a tight hug. "I'm so excited that you're my sister-in-law!"

Taking a moment to recover from my shock, I brought my arms up and awkwardly patted Leo's back. From over his shoulder, I peered at Matteo, who looked equally as horrified as I felt. Then there was the sound of a dull *thump*, followed immediately by Leo's exclamation of "Ow!" as he stepped away, rubbing the back of his head. He appeared momentarily offended, but the look quickly turned bashful at the glare he was receiving from his brother.

"Well, soon-to-be sister-in-law." He paused, still eyeing Matteo. "Future sister-in-law?" he tried again, shoulders sagging as his brother's scowl only deepened. "Oh, come on Matteo, we know it's going to happen. You're soulmates!"

Seeing that his elder sibling was not going to answer, Leo sighed. Then he turned his attention to Nina. "You're Nina?"

At her nod of affirmation, he took her hand, raising it to his lips and kissing the back of it.

"It's a pleasure."

"Piacere," Nina replied breathlessly. A pink flush crept up her cheeks, and she fidgeted, clearly flustered. Leo's eyes landed on the book that was lying abandoned on the table.

"You like to read?"

"Oh, yes. It's my favorite thing in the world," Nina replied eagerly. All traces of discomfort evaporated from her features as soon as her favorite topic was mentioned.

"Why?" He sounded genuinely confused.

"*Why*?" Nina was incredulous. "How could it not be? Books are the most wonderful thing in the world! They're filled with stories and lessons... it's like getting lost in a world that's not your own."

"But then you miss out on your own world, your own life."

"No, you don't," Nina argued, scandalized by Leo's thoughts. "Besides, what's there to miss?"

"What's there to miss?" Leo gaped at her. "There's so much to do in the world! So many places to go, so much to see, so many people to meet—"

"Yeah, people... not really my thing."

"And what is your thing?"

"Books."

"That's it?"

"Pretty much."

"How can you live like that?"

"How can you *not*?"

They were both staring at each other, as though observing an alien species.

"Well," Matteo interrupted, clearing his throat. "I'm glad to see we're all getting along."

Matteo's wry comment brought a smile to my lips that I unsuccessfully tried to fight. Seeing the toothy grin on my face, a soft look settled on Matteo's features.

"My brother has never had an appreciation for literature," he explained lightly, though he sent a pointed look in Leo's direction. "But he'll crack open a book when he needs to—like today."

There was an underlying warning in his words that even Leo seemed to detect because, looking appropriately chastised, he responded with an emphatic, "Of course!"

Nina scrutinized him skeptically, closing the book in front of her and clutching it protectively against her chest.

"My brother said you were planning on doing research today," Leo stated, dragging a chair over from the table next to us and dropping into it. The people sitting there stared at him in disbelief. Matteo quietly apologized to the small group before taking the empty seat beside me.

"I'm guessing we're looking for stuff about the Devil?"

"Matteo told you what happened yesterday?"

"Yes," Leo nodded. "Of course my brother would be the one to have a run-in with the fire demons."

"Leo..." Matteo growled.

"What do you mean?" Nina asked.

"He's a Salamander! And a highly skilled one at that. Of course, it wasn't always that way. There was this one time when we were little, he singed off our sister's eyebrows! She was only a few years old at the time. It all happened when Matteo—"

I didn't hear the rest of what Leo was saying. My mind had gotten stuck on a single word, replaying it over and over in my mind.

Salamander.

Matteo was a Salamander. One of the members of the very breed of Voktere that found pleasure in hunting, torturing, killing Vaettir like me... was my soulmate.

The blood drained from my face. I wanted to vomit.

"Oh, then there was this other time—"

"Leo!" Matteo barked. His shout grabbed my attention.

"By the Norns, if you don't shut up I'll singe *your* eyebrows off. And this time, it will be on purpose!"

"Alright, alright," Leo conceded, holding up his hands in a placating manner. "Killjoy." He crossed his arms, leaning against the table. "So, back to the research—is there anything specific we should be looking for today?"

"Not really," I answered distractedly. Nina was gazing at me worriedly, her eyes darting rapidly back and forth between me and Matteo. Ah, so she had caught on, too. "We, uh," I cleared my throat, forcing myself to focus. "We just need to find something—*anything*—that will help us figure out how to spare Venice and the people in it from the Devil and his army."

"Why don't we just fight him?"

"Uh... because he's the Devil," Matteo retorted.

"So? We outnumber him. Easy!"

"He has an army," Matteo deadpanned.

"Oh." Leo visibly deflated. "Not so easy, then."

"You think?"

"Hey, I'm just trying to be helpful here!" Leo sighed, swiping a hand across his face. "Fine. Research it is then. You said the Devil's coming back on the twenty-fourth?"

Matteo nodded.

"Then, what are we waiting for?" Leo shoved backward from the table and launched to his feet. All eyes in the café turned toward us as the wooden legs of the chair screeched against the tile floor like nails on a chalkboard. Leo's eyes glimmered with excitement, completely unaware of the attention he had drawn to us. "Let's get started!"

CHAPTER SIX

Four days. We had been browsing through books for four days, and yet we had found *nothing*. The library had shelves of tomes dedicated to myths and legends, Torcello, Venice's history... but not one of them seemed to have any information that would be useful to us.

If anything, perusing these books—in my case, perusing them *again*—only increased my frustration. It was even more evident to me now that Venice's legends were so much more than folklore. They were a single story of Venice's history. But the tale was obscured by its missing parts, its hidden details. Without them, we'd never fully understand it all—and we'd probably never find the answers we were looking for either.

As though sensing my own vexation, a loud sigh emanated from the seat next to me. I turned to look at Leo.

For the past hour and a half, he hadn't stopped fidgeting—shifting in his seat, tapping his fingers on the table, flipping book covers back and forth, banging his pencil against the notebook lying in front of him. Reading may not be his favorite pastime, but sitting still was clearly not his forte either.

Leo leaned back in his chair, pushing it onto its rear two legs as he ran a hand across his face.

"This is ridiculous," he groaned. "We're never going to find anything this way."

"Yes, we will," Nina insisted. "Everything we need is bound to be here. It's just a matter of finding the right books."

"And what if we don't find them? What if the answers we need are in a book that isn't in this library? Or what if what we're looking for doesn't even exist?"

"It has to."

"But what if it doesn't?"

"Then, we come up with a plan of our own," Nina shrugged.

"Really? And what does that plan consist of?" Curious eyes peeked at us from behind bookcases as Leo's rising voice carried across the silent space.

"Leo—" Matteo said, a hint of admonition in his tone.

"No, I want to hear this," Leo interrupted, raising his hand to silence his brother. His eyes never left Nina.

"Well... I guess we'll have to find a loophole of some sort. Something that will let us break the contract with the Devil without suffering any of the consequences."

"Wait." Leo slammed his chair back to the floor. The sound was sharp, made even louder by the silence of the library. "Your plan is to trick the Devil?"

"Not in so many words—"

"So basically, yes." Leo shook his head, snorting derisively. "We're looking for ways to trick the Devil. Great—because nothing could *possibly* go wrong with that."

"Do you have a better idea?" Nina hissed.

"Yeah. Find a plan that *doesn't* involve trying to fool someone who has the power to take my soul."

"All the books say—"

"*Ugh*!" Leo threw his hands up in exasperation. "You and all your books! How about you take your nose out of one long enough to look around and realize that this is *real life*, not a story. We're not characters in some novel—we're *real* people, with *real* problems and *real* souls that could potentially be trapped in Hell by something more malevolent than even one of your precious books could dream up. You can't keep living your life like it's one of your favorite fictional stories, because it's not. You're a Voktere, for goodness sake! You're a guardian of humankind! You need to start acting like one. If you don't, it could have dire consequences for you and everyone around you. So please, do us all a favor and get a grip on reality. Until then, save me from your so-called plans."

With that, Leo stood and brusquely stalked out of the library.

Nina stared at the space that Leo had occupied mere moments before. She looked as though she had been slapped across the face. Her mouth was hanging open, and there was a stricken, haunted look in her eyes.

"Nina—" I tried, reaching across the table. She pulled her hand back, shaking her head and casting her eyes down to the book in front of her. I looked helplessly at

Matteo, who was giving Nina a sympathetic look.

"I'm sorry for what my brother said to you," he murmured. "He's not usually like that. I don't know what got into him. He had no right to speak to you that way."

Nina's head bobbed once in acknowledgment. She sat silently for a few more seconds. Then, closing the book with a deliberate *snap*, she picked up her bag and left without saying a single word.

I was immediately uncomfortable being left alone with Matteo. Ever since I found out he was a Salamander, I was uneasy around him. Still, I had my kedja, so there was no reason he ever had to find out that I was a Daski. Our soulbond was definitely out of the question, which pained me to admit. I liked Matteo—a lot. But I couldn't let myself get too close to him. It was too dangerous... for the both of us. Besides, he hadn't made any indication that he actually wanted to acknowledge our bond. So, as long as we focused solely on our research and finding ways to save Venice, then went our separate ways in the end, there was no need for me to worry.

Right?

"Will she be okay?" Matteo asked, shaking me from my reverie. I caught a glimpse of the library door slamming behind Nina as she fled from the building.

"Eventually, yes." I sighed. "Nina, seems aloof, but she's actually quite sensitive. She hasn't had the easiest life, either. That's why she loves books so much. They give her a chance to experience new people and things without getting hurt."

"I don't know what's wrong with Leo," he growled. "He can act like a child at times, but he's never been cruel."

"It could just be the stress of the situation—after all,

it's not exactly something trivial," I commented quietly, trying to allay some of Matteo's anger. "Besides, we've all been cooped up in here for four days with no results. I think we're all feeling a bit tense and agitated right now."

"I suppose you're right." He sighed, some of the heat leaving his eyes. "I guess I had better go track down my wayward sibling."

"And I'll go find Nina—talk to her."

Matteo nodded. "Let me know if you need anything."

"I will," I promised, a feeling of warmth spreading through me at his words. "Ci vediamo dopo," I added as I gathered my own belongings and left the library.

It turned out Nina hadn't gone nearly as far as I thought she had. I found her sitting on a bench just down the street from the library. She was simply sitting there, watching blankly as people wandered past.

"Ciao," I greeted softly as I approached. She peeked up at me briefly before turning her attention back to the passersby, but it was enough for me to see the tear tracks on her cheeks. Sitting beside her on the bench, I waited patiently. I knew she would talk to me when she was ready.

Sure enough, after a few minutes of silence, she asked in a strained voice, "Am I really as naïve and bookish as he said I am?"

I sighed.

"You're not naïve. Do you sometimes get lost in the books you read? Yes, on occasion. It is, after all, the reason I ended up being painted with tomato sauce the other night." I smirked, casting a sideways glance at her. The corner of her mouth quirked up, and I cheered internally at the small victory.

"But books are what you love," I continued. "For some people it's sports, for others it's art. Then there are the weirdos like me who love history." That comment earned a much-desired chuckle, and I grinned. "But for you—it's literature. And there's nothing wrong with that.

"Do I worry that you spend too much time reading and are missing out on other parts of life? To be honest, yes, sometimes I do. Do I worry that you'll wake up one day and regret certain opportunities you've missed out on because you preferred to be reading? Yes. But I never say anything about it because I know that reading is what makes you happiest in this world."

Nina stared at her hands, nodding mutely.

"I was bullied growing up," she confessed quietly. "Reading made me feel less alone. The characters in the books I read were the closest thing I had to real friends."

"I know," I said sympathetically.

"It was easier to read than to deal with reality. Books are a safe place, where nothing can hurt you. Things are less complicated, less frightening, less fundamental to existence. Real life is much scarier. Sometimes, it's too much for me."

She looked over at me, and a pang rippled through my heart at the helplessness I saw written across her face. "I do realize that it's not good for me to get so preoccupied by books that I forget to live my own life or become disillusioned with what's going on around me. I'm trying to work on that."

"I know you are," I assured her. "And you've made leaps and bounds."

She shrugged noncommittally, sniffling as she gazed up at the gray sky. "Leo was right about my plan. It's too unrealistic, too risky."

"To be fair, everything about this entire situation is unrealistic and risky—so I think your plan might just be the best we have to work with." I watched a flock of geese soar through the clouds above us. "But if we're going to put your plan into action, we're going to need more to work with."

"Back to the library?"

I nodded, slightly amused by the eagerness in Nina's voice. "Back to the library."

At that moment, my phone pinged. Pulling it from my pocket, I saw that it was a text from Matteo.

M: Is Nina okay?

"Matteo?" Nina asked. I looked up at her, shocked.

"How did you know?"

"You get a dreamy look in your eye whenever he comes up in conversation. It's the same look you just got when you read that text," she said, nodding toward the phone in my hand. I blushed.

"I don't—"

"Don't even try to deny it, you know it's true."

I sighed, then typed back a quick message.

K: Yes. We talked. She's fine.

"He just wanted to make sure you were okay," I explained to Nina. A moment later, my phone pinged again.

M: I'm glad. I spoke with Leo.

Something about the bluntness of the message—and everything left unsaid in it—implied that the conversation had not been fun for Leo.

M: We're going to talk to people around Venice, see if anyone knows anything that could help us.

K: Sounds good. Meet back at the campo at 15:00?

M: Sì. A presto.

"Matteo and Leo are going to talk with people throughout the city to see if they can find someone who might be able to give us some answers," I informed Nina. "I told him we'd meet them back at Campo Santo Stefano at three o'clock."

"Va bene. Andiamo," she replied. By the way she practically skipped in the direction of the library, I assumed her happiness was once again restored.

CHAPTER SEVEN

Nina and I were already back in the campo by the time the campanile released its three loud tolls. We didn't have to wait long for Matteo and Leo to appear. Matteo greeted us warmly, but Leo was suspiciously quiet. He remained behind Matteo, shifting from foot to foot as he fidgeted with a small white bag in his hands.

"Sorry we're a few minutes late," Matteo stated.

"That's my fault," Leo cut in, stepping forward. "I stopped to get this." He held out the white bag to Nina. "It's a cornetto. I know it's a bit plain, but I wasn't sure what you like."

"You got me... a cornetto?" Nina gave him a perplexed look.

"I was rude to you before. I said some horrible things, and I'm sorry. Buying you a pastry seemed like the start of a good apology."

"Oh, uh, grazie," Nina stammered, caught off-guard by the thoughtful gesture. Her gaze softened as she took the bag from Leo. "That's really nice of you."

"It was the least I could do," he replied, earning a proud smile from his older brother. "I didn't mean to turn into Mr. Hyde on you." At Nina's raised eyebrow, he exclaimed, "What? Just because I don't *like* to read, doesn't mean I *don't*. The truth is, I struggled in school. Reading was always a weakness of mine, and I learned at an early age to hate it."

"I can understand that," Nina stated, tilting her head thoughtfully. "I suppose I feel the same way about interacting with people. It's kind of—" she waved a hand, searching for the right words.

"A necessary evil," I finished for her. Nina chuckled.

"Exactly."

"You don't like being around other people, either?" Matteo asked in surprise.

"It's not that I don't like it," I amended with a shrug. "I'm just... not good at it." Matteo's eyes bore into me, but I refused to meet his intense gaze.

"So, did you two find anything that could help us?" Leo questioned.

"Not a thing," I answered, grateful for the change of topic. "We had about as much luck as we've had for the past four days. What about you?"

"We came up empty-handed, too," Leo sighed in disappointment. "I thought for sure that someone would know *something*."

"It seems like people are even more tight-lipped about the situation than the books are," Matteo commented.

"The best part of our day was that shopkeeper's goat story."

"Goat story?" Nina asked, her interest piqued.

"Yeah, the signore who owns the gondola repair shop on the mainland—apparently, he closed up his shop for the day and went out gathering goats," Leo explained with a chuckle.

"Why?"

"He's going to take them to Torcello and walk them across the bridge. I have no idea why."

"Oh no," I gasped in horror.

"What is it?" Matteo's voice was filled with concern.

Ignoring Matteo's question, I instead prodded Leo for more information. "When is he taking these goats to Torcello?"

"Uh, I don't know. It sounded like he was going as soon as he had the goats collected."

"We have to get to Torcello."

"What? Why?"

"Kat, what's going on?"

I paused and took a breath, looking around at the other three.

"In my research, I came across a legend about the Rialto bridge," I began. "According to the story, the man who built the bridge struggled with its structural integrity. As soon as he built the bridge, it collapsed. So, he rebuilt it—and it fell again. Nothing he did could keep the bridge erect.

"Much like the young woman from Torcello, the man decided to call upon the Devil for help. The Devil agreed to use his powers to keep the bridge standing for all eternity; but in exchange, he had to be allowed to keep the soul of the first person who crossed it.

"The man, who was generally good at heart, didn't

want any harm to befall his friends and neighbors. So, he sent his rooster that he owned and sent it across the bridge. After all, the Devil hadn't explicitly said that the first soul to cross the bridge had to be human. And, as the rooster crossed the structure, the man assumed that he had successfully tricked the Devil and saved all those who would cross the bridge in the future.

"Unfortunately, the Devil discovered the man's deceit. To get revenge on him, the Devil tricked the man's pregnant wife into crossing the bridge. Both the man's wife and their unborn child died shortly thereafter—and the Devil took their souls.

"Wait, what does that have to do with the goats?" Leo asked, his face perplexed.

"Don't you see? When the Devil appeared on Torcello a few days ago, he demanded the payment of 'seven young souls.' Just like in the legend about the Rialto bridge, he didn't specify that the souls had to be human. There are so many other stories from around the world of people who *have* managed to trick the Devil with the souls of animals— and it sounds like that is exactly what the shopkeeper has in mind with the goats."

"Hold on, so he's going to use the goats to trick the Devil?"

"That would be my guess."

"And what happens once the Devil figures it out?"

"I'm assuming something akin to what happened with the creator of the Rialto bridge," I answered darkly.

"And in all probability, it will be worse," Matteo stated. "The Devil wanted more souls this time than he did with the Rialto bridge. Plus, he's already been spurned once by a Venetian. I doubt he'll be lenient with the punishment this time—especially since he's waited two hundred years for these souls."

"Then what do we do?" Leo inquired, eyes wide with fear.

"We go to Torcello," I responded, already setting off across the campo.

"And then what?"

"We stop the shopkeeper from sending the goats across the bridge."

"And what if we're too late for that?"

"Then I guess we're going to be getting reacquainted with the Devil sooner than expected."

"Fantastic," Leo muttered under his breath. Hurrying alongside a panicked Nina, he fell in behind me and Matteo as we raced toward a waiting vaporetto.

CHAPTER EIGHT

Dusk was settling over the Earth as Torcello came into view. The moment the boat docked at Torcello's main canal, Matteo, Leo, Nina, and I sprinted in the direction of the Devil's bridge. We pushed past the tourists that were meandering along the path, taking pictures of the unique buildings and the distant campanile. Somewhere in the back of my mind, I registered a flash of familiar white-blonde hair bobbing among the throngs of people, but I paid it no mind as we wove between the crowds.

The infamous bridge came into view after what felt like an eternity, and we all collectively froze.

At the foot of the bridge was an elderly gentleman, surrounded by seven baby goats. They bleated in confusion, scrambling around his feet; but he paid them no attention. Instead, his gaze was fixed on a younger man—presumably his son, if their similar facial features were anything to go by—who was nearing the crest of the bridge. In the hands of the latter was a lit candle.

"No!" I yelled, breaking out of my shock and rushing forward. Three sets of pounding footsteps echoed close behind me.

"Ferma!" Matteo shouted. "Per favore, ferma!"

The man on the bridge stopped, turning to look at us. But it was too late. Next to him, spinning wider and wider, grew the fiery portal that had preceded the Devil's previous visit. Sure enough, a few seconds later, the horned silhouette of the Devil emerged from its depths. I slid to a halt.

"Mio Dio," Leo whispered in horror from somewhere to my left.

"Who has summoned me?" the Devil's icy voice inquired, sending a chill through my bones. The man on the bridge trembled in fear, his shivering frame visible even from a distance. His mouth moved, speaking words murmured too quietly for any but the Devil to hear. The Devil gazed indifferently at him, then turned to look down at the elder man with the goats.

"Ah, seven young souls," he observed in a sickeningly sweet tone. "And goats, no less. Often called 'kids' when they are young, just like humans—how very clever." His red eyes flickered to the shopkeeper's wrinkled face, an ugly sneer crossing his features. "Did you really think you could fool me?"

The old man seemed too terrorized to answer. The Devil smirked.

"It would seem that Venice is in need of yet another lesson regarding the imprudence of their trickery." Then, before any of us could react, the Devil spun around and ran the tip of his pitchfork through the stomach of the shopkeeper's son. A horrid scream was ripped from his throat as the hot metal pierced his body. The older man cried out painfully upon seeing his son drop to the brick surface of the bridge, unmoving. The Devil huffed out a dark chuckle, before hurling the corpse from the bridge where it landed at the shopkeeper's feet. The old man collapsed to his knees, cradling his son's body, broken sobs of "mio figlio" tumbling from his lips.

My blood ran cold, and I felt bile rise to the back of my throat. Nina shrieked, quickly covering her mouth with a hand and turning away. Leo shielded her with his body, bringing his arms up around her as she burrowed into his chest. Matteo sucked in a sharp breath in horror.

Around us, all hell broke loose. Screaming and crying pierced the air. Some people ran off in different directions, trying to escape the grisly scene. Others stood frozen, unable to believe what they had just witnessed. Bleating goats raced between the retreating spectators, nearly tripping them in the process.

"It would seem that there are those here in Venice who think it is both acceptable and possible to deceive me." The Devil shook his head in feigned disappointment. "Well, they shall learn."

With a wave of his clawed hand, the two lines of demons emerged from the portal once more. They dispersed onto Torcello, fiery whips cracking wildly, lashing out at everyone in the vicinity. People scattered, scurrying frantically in all directions like a herd of startled cattle. They bumped into each other, running away from one Onemdi only to be driven into the path of another.

Amidst the chaos, a high-pitched squeal caught my attention. I turned, trying to identify the source of the terrorized screaming. It didn't take long. The sound was emanating from the mouth of a girl with white-blonde hair. I recognized her as the girl with the soccer ball in Campo Santo Stefano a few days ago. Now, instead of joyfully flitting from place to place, she was kicking and squirming against the grasp of a rather large Onemdi.

Without hesitation, I took off toward her.

"Katya!"

"Kat!"

I ignored the cries of my soulmate and my best friend as I flew in the direction of the demon that was dragging her toward the flaming portal on the bridge.

"No!" I shouted as I neared them, slamming my fist into the Onemdi's face, then sweeping its legs from beneath it. It tumbled ungracefully to the ground, releasing the girl as it fell.

"Let's go!" I placed a hand on the girl's back, ushering her away from the fallen demon. I ducked and dodged several tongues of fire that were flung in our direction, using my body to shield hers. We hurried across the canal path. My goal was to get her to one of the empty alleys that would allow her to escape the battle and make her way back to the vaporetto.

That plan went down the drain, though, the moment something sharp snatched my arm. I twirled around to see an Onemdi mere inches from my face. Its boney hand gripped my wrist tightly, its nails digging into my flesh. Beneath its hood, a skull with empty eyes stared down at me.

"Go!" I shouted at the girl, shoving her away from me

as I swung at the demon. Annoyed, the Onemdi easily caught my fist before my knuckles could connect with their target. Then, its other hand snaked around my throat, lifting me from the ground. I clawed at the skeletal limb, my eyes widening in fear as I gasped for air that wouldn't come. The edges of my vision began to dim.

"Kat!" Matteo's terrified voice broke through the fog clouding my mind. The next thing I knew, a bright ball of light blazed in my peripheral vision, launching in my direction. It collided with the demon, sending the creature flying across the brick pathway. I collapsed to the ground, sucking in a deep lungful of precious oxygen. Then another. I coughed, raising a cold hand to my burning throat, trying to will away the phantom pain of those bony fingers as they choked me.

As air filtered back into my body and the terror I had felt at being suffocated dwindled, I slowly regained my bearings. My eyes refocused on my surroundings again. The first thing I noticed were the tiny round beads scattered across the bricks beneath me. The flickering orange flames of battle were reflected on their pale blue surface. I stared at them. They were significant to me, but why? My brain was a bit fuzzy. It was working slower than usual.

Then it hit me. My hand flattened against the base of my neck. My fingers deftly flitted across the skin there, seeking my kedja, but my throat was bare. The necklace must have been torn off by the Onemdi when it was hurled away from me.

Oh, god.

Suddenly, Matteo appeared beside me, resting a comforting hand on my back.

"Are you alright?" he asked, concern evident in his voice. I nodded mutely, glancing over to the body of the Onemdi. I was astonished to see it on fire, the flames rapidly turning both the cloak and the skeleton inside of it to ash.

Ah, so the ball of light that hit it had been a fireball. A fireball that had been sent by Matteo.

Right. Matteo—who was a Salamander. Matteo who was currently touching me—a Daski who could no longer hide behind her kedja.

"Katya?" The worry was more pronounced this time, almost frantic. I looked up into Matteo's eyes, which retained their warmth despite the distress prevalent in their depths.

"I'm fine," I croaked, pushing myself up and away from him. As I did so, I spotted a trail of fire shooting toward Matteo's back. It streaked through the air as though in slow motion, the flames lunging hungrily for their target.

There wasn't going to be enough time to warn Matteo. The moment that realization hit me, my instincts kicked in. Shoving him aside, I launched myself in front of him, raising my hands. An icy dagger flew from my palms, meeting the strand of fire in mid-flight. Both elements collided violently before dissolving into droplets of water that rained down to the bricks below.

"We need to go!" I yelled urgently, all thoughts of the Daski-Salamander issue temporarily driven from my mind. "Where are Nina and Leo?"

"I don't know. They got separated from us," he answered. "We have to—"

Whatever he had been about to say was cut off in a

painful *oomph* as a flash of light hit him. He spiraled through the air, landing sprawled on the path a few feet away.

"Matteo!" I cried, scrambling across the short distance to his side. He was unconscious, but flames flickered intermittently from his hands. I glared up at the Onemdi approached, its whip of fire materializing in its bony grip. The creature raised the whip, the tail of flames crackling ominously.

I raised my hands, determined to protect Matteo at all costs. I could feel the familiar frostiness beneath my skin, eager to serve even after more than a decade of disuse.

As it turned out, I didn't need to attack. At that moment, something pierced the demon's torso with a sickening sound. I flinched. The object was long and thin, its surface pale and shiny in the flickering flames around us. It looked like—

Ice.

My brow furrowed in confusion. The ice hadn't come from me. I apprehensively watched the Onemdi as it towered over me and Matteo. It was frozen, almost statuesque. Its whip had fallen from its grasp, vanishing as it clattered onto the bricks below. A beat passed, and then the demon exploded, its ashes flurrying to the ground.

Behind where the demon had stood only a few seconds ago was a woman. Ferocious was the best adjective to suit her. She was tall and slim, with white-blonde hair pulled over her shoulder in a braid. Pale verdigris eyes scrutinized the world around her, their intensity enough to make even a hardened criminal cower. A bow was clutched firmly in her hand, an icy arrow prepped and nestled against the string.

She released the arrow, launching it toward an unidentified target behind me. I inadvertently ducked away from it, glancing over my shoulder to see the icy shaft piercing another Onemdi.

Rushing toward me, she yanked another arrow from the quiver on her back.

"You take care of him," she directed in a tone that brooked no argument, nodding down at Matteo before turning her eyes back to the battle unfolding around us. "I've got you covered."

I had no idea who this woman was, or why she was helping me, but what other choice did I have than to trust her?

Another arrow whizzed from her bow as I focused my attention on Matteo. He was still out cold, and flames continued to dance haphazardly from his hands. I placed a hand on his shoulder, shaking him in an attempt to wake him. Evidently, that was the wrong thing to do, as the fire in his palms flared up, shooting out at me. I dove out of the way, gawping at his still body.

"He was knocked out while fighting," the blonde woman stated as she placed another bow onto the string. "His powers think he's still fighting. They think everything's a threat, and they'll lash out at anyone or anything to protect him."

"How am I supposed to wake him up without his powers accidentally injuring or killing one of us?" I shouted, flinging myself out of the path of yet another flare that came from Matteo's hands.

"You need to calm him down—stop his powers from identifying us as a threat."

"And how do I do that?"

"How should I know?! I'm not made of fire!" she retorted, an arrow of ice targeting an Onemdi that was cornering an elderly woman.

I groaned in frustration. How was I supposed to calm Matteo, let alone wake him, if I couldn't touch him?

I knew that there was a way to calm someone through a soulbond. But that was only possible with experienced soulmates. The bond between Matteo and I was young, our relationship new. We hadn't even known each other for a week yet. I had absolutely no idea how to go about using our bond to soothe him, and there wasn't any time to experiment with it right now.

The woman fired off several more arrows in succession, the icy shafts penetrating several more Onemdi. Watching the creatures burst into drifting gray ash that resembled snow, the idea struck me.

Of course.

Matteo had been fighting fire demons all night. It was a flare cast by one of them that had rendered him unconscious. It made sense that his body would associate fire and heat with the enemy.

But ice and cold? That might just be different enough to prevent his powers from classifying me as a threat.

Or, it might trigger his magic to label me an even bigger threat than the Onemdi, considering the history of Salamanders and Daskis. I groaned, dodging another spurt of fire. This had the potential to backfire spectacularly.

Either way, it was my only option. I had to try it.

I looked down at my hands. Even with the limited light of the moon and the dancing flames coursing through the air above my head, I could make out the faint blue tinging my palms.

Taking a deep breath, I mentally prepared myself for what I was about to do. I hated using my powers. They were dangerous. But as they say, desperate times call for desperate measures.

Exhaling slowly, I placed my hands over Matteo's. The moment our skin connected, a searing heat burned my palms. Gritting my teeth, I pushed the pain to the back of my mind, concentrating all of my energy on gently caressing him with the frost emerging from my hands.

It was hard to keep control over my powers, which were screaming to attack the fire scorching my skin. Not to mention the fact that they had been locked inside of me, unable to be used, for fifteen years. But I refused to give them the freedom to react. My fear of hurting Matteo and my affection for him were too great—far greater than the strength of my powers. So, I forced the ice in my veins to be content with simply quelling the uncontrolled fire coming from my soulmate.

Ages seemed to pass. But, gradually, I could feel the heat beneath my hands growing dimmer, dwindling, smoldering, until it dissipated entirely. I sighed in relief, pulling my hands back and hiding them in my lap just as disoriented brown eyes flickered open.

"Katya?"

"Oh, good, he's awake," the archer commented from beside me as another arrow lurched from its position on her bow. "Nice going, Frosty."

I spluttered at the nickname, but my attention was quickly diverted elsewhere as a flare streaked overhead. It wasn't the red-orange of the fires of Hell, but rather the golden yellow of sunlight. I followed its trail across the dark night sky, watching as it burst directly above us. All of the Onemdi let out an inhuman screech in response. The sound was horrible, like nails on a chalkboard. I cringed, my hands flying to cover my ears.

"Well, it looks like we're done here," the woman stated, shooting off one last arrow as the demons fled back toward the portal.

"We?" I asked, lowering my hands and peering up at her.

"Hey, J, guess they didn't like my arrows, huh?" A young man, identical in appearance to our female Robin Hood, jogged over to us.

"Definitely not," she agreed with a nod. "But then, creatures of the night seldom like sunlight."

"Sunlight?"

The two blondes looked over at me. I must've looked as baffled as I felt, because the male explained, "I'm a Vali."

"And I'm an Ullr," stated the woman.

"Wait... you're Kongeligs?"

"Oh, don't give me that look," she sniped. "We're Vaettir, just like you, the human torch, and Bert and Ernie over there." She nodded at me and Matteo in turn, then jabbed a thumb over her shoulder. I followed the gesture with my eyes, spotting Nina and Leo near the canal. Judging by the parts of their conversation that made their way to my ears, the truce between them was over.

"I should've known you'd be just like your powers—it's in your nature to go with the flow. No planning involved whatsoever! Did you really think dumping water on their heads was going to work?" Leo growled in frustration.

"Oh, because tossing pebbles at them worked *so well*," Nina fired back. "Your head is as hard as the rocks you claim to control!"

Nina's outburst was almost as bizarre as the events of the evening. Not once in ten years had I heard her raise her voice even the slightest. Yet here she was, shouting brazenly at Leo, defending her bold decision to drench the demons of Hell with the frigid waters of the Adriatic.

It was ridiculous, unexpected, inexplicable—definitely in keeping with the theme of the night. Still, the fact that Nina and Leo were at each other's throats right now was evidence that they were both fine. It was also a tad amusing, and I couldn't stop the grin that spread across my face.

"I'm Janara, by the way," the blonde woman continued, drawing my attention back to her. "And this is my brother, Arun."

"We're twins," he announced.

"Thank you, Arun—clearly she *never* would've been able to figure that out," Janara remarked dryly. Arun merely shrugged.

Twins—the same eyes, the same hair...

Which reminded me—

"There was a girl, maybe seven or eight years old. She had the same hair as you."

"That was our sister, Aella," Janara confirmed with a nod.

"She's like the wind, that one," Arun commented. "Always flitting around, exploring new places, meeting new people. She's absolutely fearless."

"Which is how she ended up slipping away from me and Arun today. We were exploring Campo Santo Stefano—we're here on vacation, you see. One second Aella was right next to me, and the next she was gone. Apparently, she hopped onto a vaporetto and came here.

It took ages for us to track her down. Once we did, it was to find that she had landed herself in the middle of a battle with Hell."

"Our vaporetto docked just as the fight was starting," Arun cut in. "It took us a while to get here. We heard her screaming and tried to get to her, but some of the Onemdi weren't thrilled about two new people joining the fray. They made it difficult to get through."

"We saw you try to save her," Janara said. Her voice held a gentleness that contradicted her otherwise intrepid personality. "We thank you for that."

"It was nothing," I replied. "If it was my sister, I would hope someone would do the same."

Janara gave me a calculating look, having picked up on something in my tone that none of the others had. It must have been her keen perceptiveness—one of the traits all Kongeligs inherited from the deities. It was said they could detect lies and unravel secrets with the same ease and persistence that a bloodhound showed when tracking.

Now, with Janara's gaze fixated upon me, I was discovering just how uncomfortable the sensation truly was. It felt like I was an ant beneath a magnifying glass. Feeling the need to deflect her attention from me, I asked the question that had been nagging at me ever since I lost track of the young girl during the attack.

"Is she safe now?"

Janara and Arun glanced at each other—and in that brief exchange was a storm of anger and grief.

"No," Janara shook her head. "Arun got nicked by one of the Onemdi's whips. Aella saw it happen, and tried to avenge him." There was a sad fondness in her tone.

"She got in a solid kick to its shins," Arun stated

proudly. Then, solemnly, he added, "But that didn't hinder it much."

"The Onemdi grabbed her and disappeared into the portal before we could stop it," Janara finished bitterly.

"Then we'll help you get her back." The words were out of my mouth before I even had a chance to think about it. Not that I needed to. It was the obvious thing to do.

"Of course, we will," Matteo chimed in. I looked over at him, a flood of affection coursing through me.

"You don't have to do that," Janara protested. "We couldn't ask you to risk your lives for our family."

"Nonsense. We're helping," I insisted matter-of-factly.

"Thank you," Janara stated, the words laden with deep warmth and gratitude. "We'll have to figure out how exactly we're going to do that, but it's good to know we'll have you on our side."

"Definitely," Arun agreed. "But first, I think we could all use some rest. We'll need to be at our best if we're going to take on the forces of Hell. Come to think of it, some first aid might be good, too." He rubbed his arm, scorch marks crisscrossing his bicep.

"We have some supplies back at our apartment," I said. "You're welcome to head back there with us."

"Are you sure?" Janara asked.

"Absolutely."

"Alright," she nodded. "Then we'll meet you back at the boat." Placing a hand on her brother's shoulder, she ushered Arun away with a gentle, "Let's go."

They took a few steps before Janara paused. Glancing back at us, she gave Matteo a pointed look. "Oh, and Fireball? When we get there, you might want to take care of your girlfriend's hands."

I watched the two of them retreat down the brick path, stunned that Janara had just thrown me under the bus without a moment's hesitation. I couldn't prove it, but I was pretty sure she had done it on purpose.

"Katya?"

I turned to Matteo, who was carefully scrutinizing me.

"It's nothing," I said dismissively.

"Katya, please."

Matteo's pleading tone tugged at my heart, and I sighed in concession. Unfurling my hands, I held them out in front of me for him to see. His eyes widened.

"Katya," he breathed, reaching out for me. I yanked my hands back before he could get too close, cradling them against my chest.

"Don't touch me," I hissed. Matteo immediately backed off, raising his hands placatingly.

"I won't hurt you," he promised in a pained voice. Somewhere inside of me, our bond throbbed with concern, sadness, and guilt. When I didn't reply, he added softly, "I just want to help you."

"I'm fine," I replied tersely. Then, flinching at my own harsh tone, I added in a kinder voice, "Please, don't worry."

Skepticism was etched across Matteo's features, but he nodded in acquiescence. Relieved that I had avoided that situation—at least for the time being—I stood from the cold ground, gesturing for him to follow. "Come on. Let's go home." And together, we walked back to the boat in silence.

CHAPTER NINE

The boat ride back to Murano was odd.

Halfway back to the island, the adrenaline that had fueled Nina's fighting prowess seemed to wear off, allowing her mind to process everything that had just transpired. As the reality of the situation settled upon her shoulders, she broke down into tears. Even stranger than her breakdown in front of other people—something I had never seen happen before—was the fact that Nina all but burrowed into Leo's side as he slid beside her to comfort her. He wrapped an arm around her shoulders, whispering reassurances in her ear as her tears soaked his shirt.

Arun and Janara watched the scene with nearly identical looks of sympathy. Only when Nina's sobs dispersed and her shoulders ceased their tremendous shaking, did the twins deem the crisis to have passed and decided to enter into a quiet conversation of their own. Arun was subdued, and the look of softness and fragility on Janara's face sharply contrasted her role as the formidable warrior from earlier. A few times, I felt her calculating eyes watching me, her gaze boring into me like I was a challenging puzzle she couldn't solve. On each of these occasions, I deliberately avoided looking at her; and after a few awkward moments in which my soul felt bared for her to read like a book, her eyes would shift their focus to her brother, Nina, or some other point of interest that was—thankfully—not me.

As for Matteo... he was silent. He hadn't spoken a word since we boarded the vaporetto, nor had he even so much as glanced in my direction. And even though he was seated beside me, he had been careful to keep a respectable distance between us. Out of the corner of my eye, I could see him fidgeting—wringing his hands in a repetitive motion that spoke of underlying distress. I longed to reach out and wrap those hands in my own, hold them firm, comfort the man to whom they belonged.

But observing my own hands—the moonlight mocking me by tinging my skin a periwinkle hue in the darkness— I knew that could never happen. So, keeping my mouth closed as tightly as the hands fisted in my lap, I left Matteo to fight his internal battle alone, my heart breaking as he stared hollowly out into the black waters of the Adriatic.

In this uncharacteristic and divided fashion, the six of us stumbled into the apartment an hour later. As soon as we crossed the threshold, Nina looked around numbly as though she couldn't believe she was really back home. Then, with a mumbled, "Buonanotte," she headed to her room. The soft *click* of the door—a door that she rarely ever shut—was a clear message that she wanted to be left alone.

Arun and Leo were as loud as Nina was quiet. The two of them had started talking as soon as we docked on Murano, and they seemed to have developed an instantaneous friendship. It was hardly surprising—they were two peas in a pod. Both of them were bundles of child-like energy with huge hearts, who loved adventure and lacked mental filters.

Now, they were wrapped up in a discussion about Arun's arrows. Leo was fascinated by the fact that they were literally weaponized sunlight, and Arun was thrilled to have a captive audience with whom to discuss his most prized possessions. Oblivious to the world around them, they excitedly rushed into the den, Arun already handing over one of the golden shafts from his quiver so that Leo could examine it closer.

I sank into a chair at the table, moving as though in a daze. I felt tired, my limbs heavy. Somewhere in the back of my mind, I absently noted that Janara and Matteo had disappeared—though where they had gone, I couldn't be sure. Quite frankly, my mind was too preoccupied to care.

Several thoughts somersaulted through my brain:

First, Venice was attacked by the forces of Hell for the second time in one week. But this time, there had been consequences. A man had been murdered. A girl had been taken back to Hell by the Devil himself. And, unlike the former, she wasn't just a nameless victim—her name was Aella, and she was the younger sibling of two people who were now part of our small band of Vaettir.

Second, Matteo was a Salamander. I had already known that, of course. And it was problematic enough before the events of this evening. But now, I had lost my necklace. Which brought me to my third thought.

How to hide from Matteo. Until tonight, I had successfully concealed my identity as a Daski. But during the fight on Torcello, I had revealed my true lineage to everyone—including my soulmate, who belonged to a race of Vaettir that would track me down and kill me without a second thought.

And even if, by some miracle, Matteo didn't follow that course of action, *I* still posed a threat to *him*. Without my kedja, my powers were turned loose. I was dangerous. It was risky for anyone to be around me because of the volatility of my magic. It was a particular threat to Matteo. He and I were fire and ice—the incompatibility of our powers meant that, without the kedja to bind my magic, we were unable to so much as touch each other without causing harm. Pursuing any kind of relationship was the equivalent of a suicide mission.

So, as much as it might break my heart, what other choice did I have but to distance myself from him? What other means did I have by which to protect him? By which to protect myself?

Movement in the corner of my eye drew me out of the depths of my mind. Matteo slid into the chair beside me, setting a first aid kit on the table in front of him.

Ah, so that was where he had gone.

It was silent for a few moments as he rummaged around in the small white box. The ticking of the kitchen clock seemed louder than usual, amplified by the weight of the day's events and the inevitable conversation that I knew was coming.

"So, you're a Daski," Matteo stated calmly, as though

he was commenting on the weather. I nodded, keeping my eyes firmly affixed to the pattern of the grains in the wood of the table.

"And you're a Salamander," I countered.

"I am."

My fingers clenched and unclenched in a mute expression of anxiety. The motion caused the raw skin on my hands to pull and stretch. It stung, and I couldn't stop the wince that crossed my face.

"Can I take care of your hands?"

I turned my guarded gaze on Matteo, noting that he had pulled some burn cream and bandages from the kit and was now staring at my hands with an expression marred by guilt and horror.

"Why?"

"They're burned," Matteo explained, giving me an incredulous look. "They need to be tended to."

"It looks worse than it is," I lied, grimacing at how false my voice sounded even to my own ears. "I'm fine."

"No, you're not," he argued with a hint of frustration. "Believe me, I've accidentally burned myself with my powers enough times to know how painful it is."

"Seriously, I'm fine," I insisted, curling my hands protectively against my chest.

"Katya, *please*—" The broken plea stopped me in my tracks. Matteo's eyes glittered with pain, sorrow, longing. "I know you're hurt. Please, let me help you."

"I don't need your help."

You'll betray me. You'll hurt me. Or I'll hurt you. I won't mean to, but I will. In the end, we'll always hurt each other. It's in our natures. The words remained unspoken, but they echoed loudly in my mind.

"Katya—"

"No." I slammed a hand down on the table, gritting my teeth against the explosion of pain that erupted through the damaged limb. Shaking my head, I gathered all of my willpower to say the words that would shatter both my heart and his, but would ultimately protect us both in the long run. Forcing my voice to remain firm despite my quaking insides, I continued. "I don't *want* your help. I don't *want* whatever this relationship is that we have. *I don't want this soulbond.*"

It seemed as though those final five words rang infinitely around the kitchen. They hovered in the air, loud and grating even long after they had left my mouth. I held my breath, my heart hammering wildly in my chest.

Then I felt it. A sudden, searing pain that tore through my core—like someone had taken a ribbon and ripped it in half, the fibers straining and fraying as they were rent apart. My chest constricted, choking the air from my lungs. Tears stung my eyes. Deep inside my soul, a hollow pit formed that swallowed my entire being in a void of darkness.

Matteo's face was blank. His eyes were dull. It was like a door had slammed shut on his emotions somewhere in the recesses of his mind.

"Vabbè," he said flatly. "Mi dispiace." Setting the jar of burn salve on the table, he stood and crossed to the door, pausing with his hand on the knob. "Addio, Katya," he breathed in a hushed tone. Then, without a single glance back in my direction, he left.

The soft *snap* of the door as it closed behind Matteo resonated deafeningly around the kitchen, piercing my heart like one of Janara's arrows. For who knows how long, I simply sat staring at the door. I was in excruciating pain, yet I felt numb. Somehow, the two seemed to coexist within me, feeding off of each other. I wanted to scream and cry; but I couldn't move, couldn't speak, couldn't think, could barely breathe.

At some point, my eyes came unglued from the dark wood door, drifting to the object that I had inadvertently grabbed and was now clutching in my hand. A jar of burn cream. The same jar, in fact, that Matteo had held in his hands a short time ago. Had only a few seconds passed since then? Minutes? Hours? I didn't know. I didn't care. The amount of time mattered not anymore. All that mattered was that Matteo was gone.

The mere thought that I would never see him again sent a fresh wave of pain coursing through me. I closed my eyes against the onslaught, clenching my fist tighter around the jar.

It wasn't long before the glass grew cold beneath my fingers. Even before I looked at it, I knew that the vessel had turned to ice.

Glaring at the frozen jar, all of the hatred I felt for my powers and my heritage came bubbling to the surface. I despised being a Daski. I hated that I was a monster by my very nature. I hated that everything I touched turned to ice and cold. Above all else, I hated that I couldn't be with Matteo because of what I was—even worse, that I had to hurt him just to protect him from myself.

With a roar of rage, I hurled the jar at the door. It smashed into the wood, shattering into a million tiny pieces that rained to the floor. As the bits of ice and glass tinkled on the linoleum, I sank back into the chair. Burying my head in my hands, I gave in to my grief, allowing my tears to freely flow.

From the hall, four pairs of eyes watched sadly as silent sobs wracked my body.

CHAPTER TEN

The next few days passed slowly. All the world seemed frozen in a numb, gray state of existence. It was both a metaphorical bleakness resulting from Aella's disappearance, the Devil's threat, and the row between Matteo and myself, as well as a literal one caused by the incessant rain. No one was immune from it.

Nina was inseparable from her books. She rarely spoke, choosing instead to sequester herself away in empty corners of the apartment. Sometimes, she would make eye contact with me when passing from room to room—and the haunted expression in those jade depths revealed the impact that the Devil's visit had on her.

Although she would never admit it, Leo's absence was also affecting her. He had departed with an uncharacteristic solemnity the other night shortly after his brother.

We hadn't seen him since. And although he usually drove Nina crazy, she missed him. His personality, though the polar opposite of hers, complimented her perfectly. He brought out a side of her that I had never seen before. She became more outspoken, opinionated, and daring around him—even if not entirely by her own volition.

Similarly, Nina had an influence on Leo as well. When he was around her, he was softer, gentler, more amenable to listening and learning rather than simply acting. The two of them balanced and bettered one another. Both of them held mutual respect and admiration for the other. They even *liked* each other—despite being too proud to admit that yet.

Like Nina, Arun, too, seemed to have taken a shine to Leo. He had found in Matteo's brother a kindred spirit, someone equally as vivacious. It was hardly surprising, therefore, that when both Nina and Leo offered to house the twins for the remainder of their vacation, Arun opted to bunk with his new best friend instead of staying in the apartment with us three females. Although, if Janara's ribbing of her brother was anything to go by, he may have actually been scared off by the prospect of being outnumbered by women. It was a testament to Arun's own somber mood that Janara's joke hadn't even evoked a twitch of his lips.

As for Janara—well, she was Janara. There was no other way to describe her. She was an intriguing, enigmatic individual. Like the ocean, she had an opaque surface that hid an abundance of activity—profound thoughts, deep sentiments. Occasionally, I would catch a glimpse of... something. At times, I thought it was melancholy that I saw flickering across her features when she thought no one was looking. Other times, when I felt her watching me, I swore it was an expression of curiosity and understanding. But, whatever it was, it was always gone in the blink of an eye, too rapid and subtle to be fully deciphered.

Together, Nina, Janara, and I settled into a comfortable, though quiet, cohabitation with each other. We consumed ourselves in research as a distraction from our personal sufferings, communing for meals twice a day before dispersing once more to our separate piles of books.

Which is why I was now curled up on the sofa, sitting cross-legged with a giant tome of mythology in my lap. I stared at the pages in front of me, rubbing at my eyes as the words blurred. I had pored through the book several times already in the past several days, but had found nothing even remotely helpful to solving Venice's current predicament. It was frustrating and disheartening. No matter which books we looked at, it was always the same— the same stories, the same details, the same missing pieces.

There were less than two weeks left until the 24th. We were running out of time.

I shook my head. How had everything fallen apart in so short a time? Ten days ago, I was living contentedly within the confines of my constrained existence, confident in my solitude, with my biggest concern being if I would find enough information for my next book. Now, everything had changed.

Unconsciously, my hand moved to fiddle with my kedja, only to find my throat bare. My fingers flitted over the skin at the base of my neck.

From time to time over the years, I had often

wondered about what would happen if I were to remove the necklace that had bound my powers for the past fifteen years. I frequently envisioned ice exploding from me like the currents from a bomb blast, solidifying the world around me into frozen sculptures. Sometimes I imagined sheets of ice flying from my palms and slicing through anyone and anything in their path, leaving behind a path of destruction. On my darkest days, I pictured my magic whipping up storms of cold wind and frozen rain that catapulted the world into the next ice age. Needless to say, I was beyond relieved that the reality of unleashing my powers had been nothing at all like the nightmares of my imagination. Still, the potential havoc that my powers could cause gnawed at my gut, making me more subdued with each passing day.

The only thing that worried me more was my soulbond with Matteo. Even thinking about him sent a shock of pain through my heart. I had fallen for him—I couldn't deny that anymore. I missed him. And I hated myself for hurting him.

I could recall with perfect clarity the feelings of confusion, rejection, and heartbreak that had flooded our bond the other night. It was common knowledge that rejection of a soulbond was enough to sever a bond between two soulmates. According to all of the research that had been done on the subject, a severed soulbond was one of the most agonizing experiences to be endured. Based on what I had felt that night—both my own pain and Matteo's—I had to agree.

I closed my eyes to avoid looking at the soulmark that, though fainter, still lingered on my wrist. It was torture to see it now. The truth is, I wanted the bond with Matteo more than I had ever wanted anything else in my life. But there was too much at stake for the both of us. It was too great a gamble.

A chill against my thighs startled me from my thoughts, and my eyes flew open. Thin tendrils of frost were seeping from my fingers, creeping along the edges of the book in my lap. I immediately threw the tome onto the coffee table as though it had burned me. The crystallized ice crunched against the wood, but otherwise showed no other signs of having been disturbed. I stared at it in disgust.

"Are you okay?"

"Huh?" My eyes snapped up to find Nina observing me with concern.

"You seem a bit... upset."

"Oh." I looked down at my bandaged hands. The white gauze was loose and uneven, since I refused to allow anyone to touch me, leaving me to awkwardly wrap my hands myself. At the very tips of my fingers, a tinge of pale blue was slowly disappearing as my skin returned to its normal hue. "I'm fine."

"Are you sure?"

"Positive."

A few moments of silence passed. I could feel Nina watching me, even as my own gaze inadvertently flickered back to the now de-thawing book. Nina followed my line of sight, and as soon as she spotted the now-frosty leather cover, realization dawned on her face. She sighed, closing her own book and setting it on the table beside her.

"Stop it," she reprimanded softly.

"I don't know what you're talking about," I muttered, glaring at my hands.

"Yes, you do." When I didn't respond, she leaned forward in her chair, adding, "You're not a monster."

"You don't know that," I snapped. Pointing at my discarded tome, I continued. "Look what I did to that book! Without my kedja, even something as commonplace as *stress* makes me accidentally freeze things."

"You're just out of practice."

"It's not that, and you know it," I retorted hotly. She gave me a sympathetic look that drained all of the anger from my system. My shoulders sagged in defeat. Averting my eyes to my lap, I murmured, "You know it was never a lack of practice."

"You have to stop blaming yourself for that," she said gently.

"How can I?"

"It wasn't your fault."

"Then whose was it? Hers? Because I'm pretty sure you can't blame someone for their own death—especially when it was caused by another person."

Nina didn't reply to that, but I felt her scrutinizing me closely.

"No matter what you believe, you'll never make me see you as the monster you think you are." She paused. "You know, Matteo doesn't think you're a monster, either."

Hearing that name spoken aloud for the first time in days felt like a punch to the gut.

"Don't," I choked in a weak plea.

"Kat, he's your soulmate."

"*Was* my soulmate," I corrected brokenly.

"He still could be."

"How? You know what we are. You know that we can't be together. He knows that I'm a Daski. He's not going to want to be with me. But even if he did still want me, even if there was a chance that we could be together... do you honestly think he'd want anything to do with me after what I said to him the other night? Do you think he'd want to be with me knowing that we'd have to hide it from the world?"

"Yeah, I do." Nina sighed at the skeptical look I gave her. "The other night, when you broke up with Matteo—"

"I didn't break up with him," I interrupted, then shifted uncomfortably as Nina quirked her brow in disapproval. "I mean, we weren't dating."

"Well, then, when you ended your *friendship* with Matteo—" She gave me a pointed look, and I nodded in acceptance of her modified wording. Not that I would've interrupted her again after the glare she had just given me. "—what did you feel?"

"Pain," I answered regretfully.

"Just yours?"

"No," I shook my head. "Matteo's, too."

"Exactly. He knew you were a Daski, and still he wanted to help you, to heal you, to be with you. He still wanted the bond even *after* he found out about what you are. Don't you see? To him, you weren't a Daski, you weren't an inferior breed of Vaettir, you weren't a monster. You were the girl he fell in love with." Then, for good measure, she added, "And *yes*, he's in love with you— I could see it in the way he looked at you whenever you weren't looking. That man *adores* you. Even Leo said so. Apparently, Matteo talks about you—and how he feels about you—a lot."

I didn't answer. I couldn't. Emotions churned in me like an angry sea, and any words that I wanted to say got lost in the swells and waves. Nina tilted her head as she observed me, her eyes filled with compassion.

"Look, I know that none of this is easy for you. And I understand why you pushed Matteo away, why you're pushing *us* away. But you need to have a little faith—in me, in Matteo... in yourself. Yes, you're a Daski. But you're not a lower caste of Vaettir, as so many claim you are. Nor are you a monster, like so many other Daskis are. Your kindness, your generosity, the unending love and support you show everyone around you proves that beyond a shadow of a doubt.

"So, you shouldn't be shocked that the Norns would make an exception for you," she continued, gesturing toward my left wrist and the soulmark that was peeking out from beneath my sleeve. "It sounds cliché and naïve, and I know you don't believe in destiny, but I think everything happens for a reason. Fate tied you and Matteo together in the most intimate way possible, despite the fact that no other Daski on record has ever been gifted with a soulbond. That wouldn't have happened if the two of you weren't meant to be with each other.

"I'm not telling you any of this is going to be easy—controlling your powers, repairing your relationship with Matteo, figuring out the details and quirks of your bond. There are going to be really hard moments. It's going to take work—every relationship always does. But it doesn't have to be as difficult as you're making it, and it definitely doesn't have to be impossible."

Her speech concluded, Nina leaned back in her chair. "Just think about it," she suggested, raising an eyebrow at me in silent encouragement. Then, picking up her book, she opened it to the page on which she had left off and resumed reading, leaving me to process her words in silence.

CHAPTER ELEVEN

It was quiet when I woke up. Too quiet.

One of the first things I learned upon moving in with Nina was that mornings were her time to do... well, pretty much everything she postponed while reading in the afternoons and evenings. As such, I had long grown accustomed to waking up to the low sounds of rustling and banging as Nina went about her business in various rooms of the apartment.

There was none of that familiar noise today, though.

"Nina?" I called, leaving my room and moving down the hall. Checking her room, I found it empty. The bed was made, so clearly Nina was already awake and had been for a while.

"Nina?" I asked the silent apartment again as I entered the kitchen. There was still no answer, the room vacant.

Peeking into the den, I saw that it, too, was deserted. With my hands on my hips, I let out a low hum of confusion just as my eyes landed on a piece of paper lying on the table. Picking it up, I easily recognized Nina's tilted scrawl.

Kat,
I had to leave for a while. I can't tell you where I'm going, or why. I'm fine though, so please don't worry. I'll be back as soon as I can.
- Nina

I stared at the words, rereading them. Despite the reassurances in the short note, a pit of worry grew in my stomach. This wasn't like Nina. She was organized, meticulous, a planner. In the nearly ten years I had known her, not once had she done something as impulsive as this—taking a spontaneous trip to an undisclosed location for an indefinite amount of time. Nor was it like her to be so secretive.

Questions whirled loudly through my head as I sat at the table, absently twirling the small scrap of paper between my fingers. Where in the world had she gone? Why did she take off so suddenly? And why couldn't she tell me the reason for her trip?

"What did it do to you?"

I spun around in surprise, startled from my contemplative state. Janara was leaning against the doorframe, her arms crossed loosely across her chest.

"What do you mean?"

"The wall," she clarified, nodding in the direction of said object. "It must have done something horrible to offend you judging by the glare you're giving it."

I snorted, Janara's familiar sarcasm easing some of my tension.

"It didn't do anything to me. Just an innocent victim, I suppose."

As I turned back to the table, I felt Janara's eyes boring into my back. The ticking of the clock filled the silence for several long seconds before Janara's light footsteps interspersed the steady rhythm. A moment later, she sank into the chair beside me.

Pulling an arrow from the quiver hanging on the back of her seat, she rolled it between her fingers, analyzing it closely. Then, whipping out her pocket knife, she started sharpening the tip of the icy shaft.

"What's wrong?"

I glanced at her from the corner of my eye, biting my lip.

"Nina's gone," I answered. "She went... *somewhere*. She didn't tell me where, or for how long. She just left me this note." I held up the paper in question, a small corner of it tinged blue with ice.

"Does she disappear like that often?"

"No, that's what's so concerning about this."

"Ah. So, you're worried about her?"

"Yes. Disappearing like this is so unlike her."

"Do you think she's in danger?"

"I don't know. She told me not to worry, but..." I trailed off.

"If she told you not to worry, then you need to trust that. Have a little faith in her."

I stared at Janara. Her words mirrored those that Nina had spoken to me the previous night. I tended to forget she was a Kongelig—until she did things like that. Did she even know she was doing it, or was intuition the equivalent of breathing for Kongeligs?

I sighed, shaking my head to clear it of my mental digression.

"You're right," I said. "In all the time I've known Nina, she's never steered me wrong. Not once. So, if she can't tell me where she went or why, then I trust her judgment. She'll tell me when she can. If she tells me that she's fine, and that I shouldn't worry, then I trust that she's being honest. And if she tells me that she'll come back when she's able to, then I believe her."

I paused, tilting my head as I thought about my absent friend.

"Besides, as bookish and aloof as she might seem at first, she's remarkably strong and incredibly adept at just about everything she does—probably even more so than she realizes at times. I know for a fact that she's more than capable of handling anything that comes her way. She'll be fine."

And as I spoke the words, I found that I actually believed them. Somehow, I knew that Nina would be okay.

"Good," Janara stated. She whittled away a few more slivers of ice, the tip of the arrow becoming more defined with each stroke of the blade. She held it at arm's length, examining her work for a moment before continuing to carve away at the point. "Well, now that we have *that* settled... care to tell me why you ran away from your soulmate?"

I gaped at her, my mouth moving soundlessly before I regained enough of my bearings to snap it closed. I had certainly *not* been expecting that turn in the conversation. I wasn't even sure that I was ready to discuss it. It was too painful.

So, making a weak attempt at denial, I insisted, "I didn't run away from him."

Janara paused in her whittling, her verdigris eyes rising to meet mine. She quirked a skeptical eyebrow at me.

"You know, you suck at lying."

There was no hostility or judgment in her tone. Her words were merely the voicing of a truth that I had been aware of for quite some time. Yet, it was also something more than that. It was a pledge of support—Janara's way of telling me that she could see through my façade and refused to abandon me to fight my battles alone.

A warm feeling of gratitude blossomed in my chest. And suddenly, in the patient silence with which Janara waited for my answer, it felt easy to let the words spill unimpeded from my lips.

"He's a Salamander, and I'm a Daski."

"So?"

"What do you mean 'so?'" I asked incredulously. "Surely, as a Vaettir, you've heard the stories of Salamanders and Daski. We're the two groups of Vaettir who can't be together. Our powers are too incompatible. Plus, we're from two different races. He's considered an honorable warrior by Vaettir society; I'm looked at like a criminal. Not to mention the fact that Salamanders are notorious for hunting Daskis. The list of reasons that our relationship should be impossible is endless. Yet, somehow, we've been bound together as soulmates."

"Exactly, you're soulmates. That kind of bond is more powerful than any other. If the Norns decided to unite the two of you with such a connection, then there has to be a way to make it work even in spite of your Vaettir identities."

"Nina said something similar to me last night," I replied with a small chuckle. Something in my voice must have given me away though, because Janara frowned.

"You don't believe her?"

"It's not that, exactly," I said slowly.

"Then what is it?"

I sighed. "It's our Vaettir powers. Our magic is at odds with each other—fire and ice. Knowing Matteo, he'd overlook the race difference in a heartbeat. The Salamanders' hatred of Daskis? That might be a bit harder. But our powers? They're dangerous together. We found that out the hard way." I fiddled with the sloppily wrapped bandages on my hands.

"You're afraid he'll hurt you again?" Janara inquired.

"What? No! Of course not," I exclaimed. "Well, not in the way you're thinking. This wasn't his fault." I held up my hands for emphasis.

"But...?"

"But the other night showed me what *could* happen if one of us were to lose control of our powers. And, let's face it—between me and him, I'm the one most likely to cause a mishap. It's in my nature."

"Says who?"

"Everyone," I muttered miserably. "Everything I've ever heard or read about the Daskis says that we're monsters that are naturally disposed to cause destruction and pain. That's why we're targeted by the Vaettir—by Salamanders."

"Oysters."

"What?"

"Oysters," Janara repeated. My brow furrowed in confusion, part of me worried that she had suddenly lost her sanity. Catching the look on my face, she sighed, tucking the penknife back in her pocket.

"Look, I was just like you once," she began, fiddling with the arrow in her hands. "I don't think I need to tell you that Daskis and Ullr are very similar—we're both gifted with powers of ice. And yes, it *is* a gift," she added pointedly at my look of disbelief. "Unfortunately, we're also both seen by history and society in the same way—as monsters with hearts as cold as the ice flowing through our veins. It doesn't help that many Daskis and Ullr live up to that reputation. But there are always exceptions to every rule. The descriptions of callousness and criminality don't apply to all Daskis and Ullr—least of all to you and me.

"I grew up hearing stories of the Ullr who became greedy, tyrannical, bloodthirsty rulers. From the moment I learned that I was an Ullr, I was plagued with the fear that I would one day become like them. I thought it was my destiny to be a monster that was just as vicious and ruthless as the ones in the legends. I didn't think I had a choice in the matter.

"So, to protect my family, I started closing in on myself. I hid from my parents and my brother, and would lock myself away in my room whenever they were around. My parents thought I was just anti-social. But when I was assigned my mentor—as all Kongelig are when they turn thirteen, to help them prepare for their future leadership roles—he recognized my actions for what they were—fear.

"All of the hatred I felt at being an Ullr built up until I broke down crying in the middle of our lessons one day. I told him everything—about how I was hurt by being rejected by the Kongelig community, about how I didn't want to turn out to be like the Ullr from the stories, about how I was afraid of hurting my family, about how much it hurt to always have to hide from everyone. He was an Ullr, too, so he understood where I was coming from. He also revealed to me that he had been just as distressed about his identity when he was younger. He then shared with me an important maxim that he had learned from *his* mentor, which helped him to overcome his fears and embrace who he was.

"He said that Ullr were oysters. They all look the same to people observing them. Most oysters are slimy and, quite frankly, disgusting. Don't ever eat one of those things." She shook her head, scrunching her nose in distaste. "But there are other oysters that, when opened, contain pearls—pearls that are beautiful, valuable, and rare by their very nature. And some Ullr, he said, were like those pearls. They were special because they chose to use their powers for *good*—to help people, to make the world a better place. He told me that he and I were two of those special Ullr.

"At first, I didn't quite understand what he was trying to say. I thought he was just senile. But then, a few months later, my family was attacked by a Varme. Our father was the only one home with us at the time, and it killed him first before setting its sights on us. My brother tried to fight it off, but Varme are one of the rare demons that thrive on heat and light—so Arun's efforts had no effect other than to anger the Varme further. It tried to kill him, and that was the moment when everything changed for me. Suddenly, my biggest fear was no longer that I would hurt my brother, but rather that I would lose him. It pushed me into action, and I killed the Varme with an arrow through the heart."

Janara toyed pensively with the arrow in her hands before continuing. "That day made me realize that my mentor had been right. I wasn't like the other Ullr that myths and legends told us about. I was different. Oh, of course, I *could* be a monster if I wanted to—killing the Varme proved that I had the ability to do horrid things with my powers. But I didn't *want* to. I didn't want to be a monster, I didn't want to hurt people, I didn't want to use my powers for malevolent purposes. And I never did—not until there was a direct threat to my family that left me with no other option.

"You see, I *choose* to be who I am. My genetics don't dictate that. Once I realized that, I finally understood what my mentor had been trying to tell me: that I didn't have to be afraid of myself, because I wouldn't *let* myself become someone—or something—that needed to be feared.

"And that's what makes you different, too. I'm sure you've been told all your life that, because you're a Daski, you're evil. But I've seen the way you treat other people—the way you protected my sister and Matteo during the fight in Torcello. I've seen how much you struggle with your identity, and the lengths you're going to—including putting yourself through extensive physical and emotional pain—just to protect the people around you. What you need to understand is that, just like me and just like my mentor, you are a pearl—a pearl in a sea of oysters. You're not going to hurt anyone—at least, not anyone who doesn't deserve it—with your powers. I *know* you won't, because you *choose* not to.

"You need to trust yourself." She gazed at me with eyes that were firm, but gentle. "It's only when you do that, when you learn to embrace your powers as a part of who you are, that you will finally be free from the fear. And once you are—once your doubts and anxieties are behind you—you'll shine brighter and fly higher than you could've ever imagined.

"Don't deny yourself—or Matteo—the happiness you both deserve. Like I said earlier, the Norns wouldn't have joined the two of you together with such an intimate and permanent bond if your relationship wasn't meant to be. You may have only known each other for a short time, but Matteo cares deeply for you, and he trusts you. I saw it that night in Torcello. I trust you, Nina trusts you, my brother trusts you, and I'm pretty sure Leo trusts you, too—though dealing with him is like wrangling cats, so who really knows." She shrugged dismissively, and I choked out a watery laugh. A small smile appeared on her lips, and she finished in a soft voice, "Now, you just need to hop on board with the rest of us and trust yourself."

Then, as though she hadn't just delivered what was perhaps the most profound speech I had ever heard, Janara turned back to the arrow in her hands. She peered closely at the fletching, humming in disapproval as she pulled out her knife to make a few adjustments to the icy feathers.

"And as for the Salamander-Daski thing?" she added off-handedly. "I wouldn't worry too much about it. I can tell Matteo's not like other Salamanders, just as you're not like other Daskis. He's not going to hurt you that way. Besides, if he was, he would've done it already."

She shook her head. "If you ask me, this whole 'class war' that exists between the different races of Vaettir is ridiculous. It's based on prejudices and generalizations that are more harmful than anything. I've met Kongelig who were worse than any Daski, Voktere who fought dishonorably or were too cowardly to fight at all, and a Daski—" she pointed the arrow at me. "—who was more noble than any so-called elite Kongelig. So really, it's all a bunch of nonsense. Forget about it all. I have. And before you start worrying about it, I'm pretty sure Matteo has, too. He's smart enough to know that you can't judge a single person by the whole group."

I sat in silence, replaying Janara's words over in my mind. Yes, she had voiced many of the same sentiments that Nina previously had—but they had a different impact coming from someone with similar powers, someone who knew what it was like to be labeled a monster, someone who understood what it was to fear yourself.

She was right. Everyone in our little clan trusted me—except for myself. Granted, that wariness stemmed from a legitimate cause. After all, I hadn't always feared myself. In fact, there was a time when I once viewed my powers as the gift that Janara claimed they were. But then, a single accident had changed all of that.

The question was: did a single mistake when I was ten warrant a lifetime of self-hatred and unhappiness? Or, was it possible to try to move past that and start anew?

Was I even capable of that at this point?

I caught Janara glancing at me occasionally from the corner of her eye, as though checking to make sure that she hadn't somehow broken me. Her continued presence was comforting. It served as a reminder that I wasn't alone. I never would be if she and Nina—and Matteo, I reminded myself—had anything to say about it.

And that was how I knew that everything would be

alright. Maybe I couldn't change the past, and maybe I wasn't entirely convinced that I could be trusted... but I *could* choose my path for the future.

And I wanted that path to begin with trusting my friends—as well as their faith in me.

"Janara?" I asked hesitantly. She raised her head to look at me. "Do you mind if I step outside for a few minutes? I have a call to make."

"Not at all," she replied with a shake of her head, a wide smile stretching across her face. "Take as long as you need."

I nodded in appreciation before flinging myself from the chair and rushing across the kitchen. Grabbing my jacket from its hook by the door, I turned back to face Janara.

"Janara?"

"Hmm?" she hummed in acknowledgment, still whittling away at her arrow.

"Thank you."

I didn't know how to adequately express the gratitude flowing through me in words. Thankfully, Janara seemed to understand. She looked up at me, and her lips curved into a small, lopsided smile.

"You don't need to thank me," she stated warmly, jutting her chin in the direction of the door. "Just go find your happiness."

Not needing to be told twice, I flung the door open and rushed out of the apartment. Flying down the stairs, I slipped my phone from my pocket and scrolled through the contacts, searching for my soulmate's name.

CHAPTER TWELVE

Of all the things I had done in my life, I never dreamed that knocking on a door would be one of the most terrifying.

Thirty minutes ago, I had called Matteo to ask if we could talk. As soon as I hung up, I had made my way across Murano to his apartment. The walk seemed to simultaneously take both the blink of an eye and an eternity. By the time I arrived at Matteo's door, my stomach was in a knot and my brain cells were a tangled mess. And despite all the time I'd had to think about it on my walk to his home, I had absolutely no idea what I was going to say.

Which is why I had now been standing on the other side of the threshold for several long minutes, chewing anxiously on my bottom lip and desperately fighting the urge to flee for the hills before anyone knew I was there.

The only thing that kept my feet firmly planted in place

was the fact that Matteo was on the other side of the door.

Matteo, who was my soulmate.

Matteo, who I had hurt terribly.

The mere thought made my stomach churn. It was made worse by the very real possibility that the damage I had wrought might not be reparable.

Still, Matteo had agreed to talk with me. That had to be a good sign, right?

Nevertheless, it took all of the courage I had to finally raise my shaking hand to the door and signal my arrival with three knocks.

I flinched as the solid raps echoed through the empty hallway. My pulse raced. Taking a deep breath, I released the air slowly, trying to dispel the wave of nausea that assaulted me.

Then the doorknob jiggled, and as the door swung open, I couldn't help but hope that a black hole would suddenly open up beneath my feet and suck me into it.

It took a moment for me to register the person standing on the other side of the threshold, but when I did, I let out a sigh of relief.

"Hi, Arun."

"Katya, hi!" he exclaimed. His cheery tone was juxtaposed by his drawn features. "How are you?"

"I'm alright," I shrugged. His eyes softened in understanding as they roamed over my own pinched features. "What about you?"

"As well as can be expected," he answered honestly, a dark shadow crossing his face.

"We'll find her, Arun," I reassured him. "Somehow, someway, we'll find Aella and get her back."

"Of course, we will," Arun responded with feigned

confidence and a bright grin. "Janara and I have been working on a few more theories about how to do just that. Actually, that's where I'm heading now."

"Oh, you're leaving?" As relieved as I was that he wouldn't be there to witness my conversation with Matteo, I also felt a twinge of disappointment. It would have been nice to have a friend there for moral support.

"Yeah. Janara just called me a few minutes ago—we're going to meet at the café and talk through our new plans over lunch."

Wait. A few minutes ago? That meant she called him just after I had left our apartment. And I knew for a fact that there were no new theories—Janara had told me as much last night. Putting two and two together, gratitude swelled up inside of me. I couldn't be certain, but it seemed like Janara was trying to occupy her brother so that Matteo and I could have some privacy for our discussion. I had to remember to thank her for that later.

"Which is great, because I'm *starving*," Arun continued. He leaned towards me, lowering his voice as though disclosing an intimate secret. "Matteo may love food, but between you and me, he's much better at eating than cooking. The things he does to food... it should be a crime!"

I giggled at the scandalized expression that crossed his face. Shaking his head, Arun's brow furrowed in puzzlement. "I have no idea how Leo has survived it for as long as he has. I've only been here for a few days, and already I'm wasting away."

"Well, we can't have that," I retorted dryly.

"Definitely not. After all, I'm the fun twin—my sister's life would be dreadfully boring without me." Though it was said in jest, there was a hint of truth in his words, as well as an underlying current of fondness stemming from the knowledge that he truly was an integral part of Janara's life.

"Speaking of which..." He glanced down at his watch, muttering a nearly inaudible explicative. "I'd better get going, otherwise I'll be late. And I'd really rather not face J's wrath if I can help it. Between you and me, she can be pretty scary when she wants to be."

"Yes, she certainly can be," I chuckled in agreement, recalling the ferocity she exhibited when I first met her on Torcello. Arun's verdigris eyes sparkled in amusement as I added playfully, "We wouldn't want you to get on her bad side."

"Exactly." He tapped his nose three times knowingly. "I'd best be on my way, then." With that, he slipped past me, offering a quiet farewell and a quick wave before taking off down the hall.

I watched his retreating form, shaking my head fondly. Sometimes it astounded me that Janara and Arun were twins. She was so calm, collected, and serious. But he was... well, he wasn't quite as much of a whirlwind as Leo, but he was close. If it weren't for his appearance, I would swear that he was actually Leo's brother, not Janara's. What an odd twist of fate it would be if we were to discover that one of them really had been switched at birth...

"Katya?"

My thoughts skidded to a halt, and my breath caught in my throat. I slowly turned around, coming face-to-face with Matteo. Dressed in an old gray hoodie and faded blue jeans, he was standing just inside the doorframe, regarding me with a circumspect gaze. Beneath mussed hair and the familiar black-framed glasses, dark circles rimmed his eyes.

But despite the wariness and exhaustion, there was no hostility in his demeanor. That, at least, was a good sign. Perhaps not all hope was lost.

"Ciao," I breathed. Then I frowned, unsure how to proceed beyond that simple greeting. There was no point in asking how he was—I had felt his pain that night I rejected our bond; he had probably been suffering just as much as I had since then.

"So, you said on the phone that you wanted to talk?"

Apparently, he had recognized my troubled musings and decided to take pity on me. If possible, the pit of guilt in my stomach grew wider. Even with everything I had put him through, Matteo was still showing me the same kindness and consideration that he had when I first met him. My throat burned at the realization, and I swallowed thickly.

"Uh, yes, I did," I began, rubbing at my arm uneasily. "I wanted to apologize for how I treated you the other night. I didn't mean any of what I said. The truth is: I *do* want this soulbond with you. I just..." I sighed, my shoulders sagging. "There are so many reasons why a relationship between us might not work. I was scared, and I thought I was doing the right thing for both of us by pushing you away."

Shaking my head regretfully, I continued. "But I was wrong. I should've talked to you about it. I should've trusted you. I realize that now." In a more tentative voice, I finished, "And, if it's not too late, I'd really like to try to fix things between us by talking things through with you *now*."

I shifted awkwardly from foot to foot in the silence that followed. My eyes flickered to the door, the doorframe, the floor, the wall—anywhere that wasn't Matteo. I could feel his eyes boring into me, scrutinizing me. Mentally, I steeled myself for the worst.

But then, to my relief, Matteo's lips twitched into a ghost of a smile.

"I'd like that," he said softly, stepping aside to allow me into his apartment. "Come in."

Despite the circumstances surrounding my presence there, I immediately felt comfortable in the small flat. The kitchen alone exuded hospitable balminess. Tan walls lined with dark walnut cabinets surrounded the room. An eggshell white floor, interspersed with diamond-shaped emerald designs, accentuated the various plants scattered along the counters and window ledges. Rich yellow lighting filled the atmosphere with a subtle coziness.

It was like the hand of Mother Nature herself had decorated the space.

Matteo must have seen the intrigue on my face as I observed the kitchen, because he explained, "As an *uomo della terra*, Leo is most comfortable in nature. It helps calm him—and yes, believe it or not, he can actually be calm. So, when we moved in, we filled the apartment with plants and earthy colors."

I gave Matteo a curious look. "An *uomo della terra*?"

"It's a term Leo made up to refer to himself and other Vaettir like him. He wasn't happy that the ancients called them gnomes. That may have partially been my fault, though."

Suddenly, looking like a kid who had just gotten caught with their hand in the cookie jar, he rubbed at the back of his neck. "Once, when we were children, I tried to dress him up as a gnome—but the kind from modern fairytales, not the traditional earth Vaettir. Leo tolerated the shirt and the pointy red hat, but he drew the line at the fake beard. Since he wouldn't willingly wear it, I decided it would be a good idea to glue it on him while he was asleep. When he woke up... well, I had a black eye for a week after that."

I pressed my lips together, struggling to fight the smile spreading across my face. A familiar sparkle, full of humor, flickered in Matteo's eyes. I gazed, captivated, into those glimmering depths that I had missed so much over the past few days. They were even more beautiful, even more breathtaking, even more precious to me now. I thought I'd never see them again...

A piercing whistle broke me from my daze. A warm blush crept up my cheeks as I became aware of the dreamy look on my face. I tucked a strand of hair behind my ear in embarrassment as Matteo hurried across the kitchen to remove the screaming kettle from its burner.

"I'm making tea. Would you like some?" Matteo inquired from his place in front of the stove.

"I would love some."

"Coming right up." He moved to a cabinet at the other end of the long counter, gesturing toward the table beside me as he added, "Make yourself at home."

I took a seat, observing his fluid movements in silence for a few seconds. Soon, though, the comfort I had felt a few moments ago dissipated, and restlessness crept over me again.

"So," I began, clearing my throat. "How's Leo?"

"I wouldn't know." Matteo's tone took on a hard edge. "He's gone."

"Gone?"

"He left sometime last night. I woke up this morning and found that note pinned to my door." He nodded toward a small piece of paper lying at the center of the table. I picked it up, my eyes scanning it. Other than the spiky handwriting, it was identical to the one that Nina had left for me.

"He didn't tell me where he went, or why," Matteo continued, his voice filled with rare agitation. "He just told me he'd come back eventually."

"So did Nina," I commented.

"What do you mean?" He spun around to face me.

"Nina disappeared last night, too. I woke up this morning and found a note from her. Actually, it was exactly the same as this one," I stated, waving the note for emphasis.

"Really?"

I nodded, and Matteo puffed out a breath. "Well, at least that means that they're most likely together—*wherever* they are."

I hummed in agreement. "It's kind of funny—I never would have thought that they, of all people, would take off together." Pausing, my brow furrowed. "You don't think they killed each other, do you?"

Carrying the two cups of tea to the table, Matteo released a breathy chuckle.

"I hope not. I'm not sure where we'd hide the bodies." I snorted, murmuring a quiet word of appreciation as he set one of the cups down in front of me. Watching the thin wisps of steam curl out of the cup, I bit my lip.

"So, what do we do?"

Matteo sighed, taking a seat across from me. "There's not much we *can* do—not without knowing where they are."

"Do you think it has something to do with Torcello?"

"It might. We'll just have to wait until they get back to find out." He took a sip of his tea, eyeing me over the rim of his cup. "Speaking of Torcello, though…"

Hesitance tinged his tone, and the amusement that had glittered in his eyes a moment ago was replaced by something somber and guarded.

"What happened that night, Katya?"

"Well, we were attacked by the Devil—"

"That's not what I meant, and you know it." His eyes bored into mine with an intensity that made me feel completely exposed. "Katya, please."

His voice was gentle, but it held a desperate plea for truth—for an honest explanation that would help him understand why I had so cruelly broken his heart. My shoulders sagged in defeat. It was time to stop stalling. I had to tell him everything.

"I was afraid," I confessed in a small voice.

"Afraid—why?"

"Matteo, you're a Salamander. I'm a Daski. We're supposed to hate each other."

"You thought I'd kill you." It wasn't a question.

"Eventually, yes. I mean, why wouldn't you? Most Salamanders take great pleasure in hurting, torturing, slaughtering Daskis."

"I'm not most Salamanders," he answered quietly. "Katya, I'd *never* do something like that. Not to you, or any other Daski," he swore passionately. "I've always been ashamed of being a Salamander because of the way so many of them treat Daskis. We're supposed to be an honorable, respectable race," he spat bitterly. "The last time I checked, it was neither honorable nor respectable to find sport in harming another living being. I've never taken part in that, and I never will."

"Even though we're monsters?"

He froze, shaking his head. "Not all of you are."

"Most are."

"Some aren't." He nodded in my direction. "You, for instance." He paused. "I've found it's best to take each person for who they are, not judge them based on the race or class they belong to."

"Janara said you'd feel that way."

"She did?"

"Mm-hmm," I hummed.

"Well, she is a Kongelig, after all." He smirked. "She knows things."

I snorted. "Yeah. Her powers of perception freak me out a little."

"You and me both. She's better at it than most. It's like she can read minds."

"Exactly!" I scrunched my brow in thought. "Is that normal for Kongeligs? Or is that just her?"

"I have no idea," he shrugged. "I've never met another Kongelig before." Lowering his voice and leaning forward, he whispered conspiratorially, "I think it's just her."

His twitching lips gave him away, and I chuckled. "Probably."

A comfortable silence settled over us, stretching on for several minutes.

"You still haven't answered my question, you know."

"Huh?" I nearly choked on the mouthful of tea I was swallowing.

"Being afraid of what I would do to you once I found out you were a Daski at least partly explains why you rejected our bond." I cringed at the words. It sounded so much worse when spoken out loud. "But it doesn't explain everything."

"Wh—what do you mean?" I stammered.

"Katya, you wouldn't even let me near you. Your hands were hurt. I wanted to help you. But you acted like even the slightest touch would burn you!"

"It would've."

"What?" Matteo looked like he'd just been slapped.

"No! Not me, you! Urgh," I groaned at my own verbal incompetency, swiping a hand across my face. "I'm sorry, that didn't come out right. What I meant to say was that *you* might've been burned. Well, frost-bitten. Iced? There's really not a good word for it, is there?" I bit out a nervous laugh. "I mean, yes, you could've possibly burned me. Actually, you already had. Not that it was your fault, though! You were unconscious. You could hardly know what you were doing. So, really, it was the Onemdi's fault, since they're the ones who attacked us. And yes, there was a small part of me that was worried about that, I guess. But it wasn't my main concern. I wasn't even really thinking about it at the time. Well, maybe I was, just a little. But really—"

"Katya!" I snapped my mouth shut at Matteo's sharp tone. He pinched the bridge of his nose, his face softening. "Katya, stop. You're rambling."

"Oh, right. Sorry." I flushed in embarrassment.

"Don't apologize. Just—give it to me slow, so I can keep up." He blew out a long breath. Then, in a strained voice, he asked, "So, you wouldn't let me touch you because you were afraid that I'd hurt you with my powers again?"

"No! Yes? Sort of," I admitted in shame, ducking my head.

"Explain that to me," he pushed gently.

"We're polar opposites, Matteo," I explained in a voice that was barely louder than a whisper. "You're fire, and I'm ice. It's dangerous for us to be together. Our powers, by their very nature, seek to destroy each other." I bit my lip. "You should know the stories better than anyone—the tales of the Salamanders and Daskis who have killed each other with just a single touch."

"I know the stories, sì. But I figured our situation would be different, all things considered." He rolled up his sleeve, revealing our familiar soulmark. The colors were duller now, the mark slightly faded; but it was still there. "I was willing to give our bond a try, despite the risks. I thought it was worth it."

I was willing to try. I thought it was worth it. Matteo's use of the past tense didn't go unnoticed by me. A gaping black hole opened in my heart. My throat burned. My vision blurred.

"I thought you did, too," he continued. "We spent some wonderful time together—at least, I thought we did."

"We did," I croaked, desperate to assure him of my mutual feelings for him.

"But then, after that fight on Torcello, everything changed. I get that you were afraid of me, and I know that I physically hurt you. True, it wasn't my fault," he amended quickly, holding up a hand to stop my protest. "But the fact is, my powers still hurt you. I can't deny that. And I'll regret that for the rest of my life." He shook his head sadly. "But there's something else. There was another reason you didn't let me help you that night. What was it? What made you change your mind about me?" His voice cracked. "Why did you reject our bond?"

I swallowed thickly, squeezing my eyes shut against the tears threatening to fall. My voice almost inaudible, I answered weakly, "I was trying to protect you."

"Protect me? From what?"

"From myself."

Matteo frowned. "I don't understand—"

"Matteo, if I was *only* afraid of you hurting me—which I'm not... at least, not anymore—then I would give our relationship a shot. To me, it would be worth the risk. It *is* worth the risk. But you're forgetting that *I* could also potentially hurt *you*, and that's not a gamble I'm willing to take."

I sighed, absently running a finger around the rim of my teacup. "I'm a Daski. My powers are the most volatile of all the Vaettir. And they're dangerous—*I'm* dangerous. Oh, I may lack the callousness and maliciousness of most Daskis, but that doesn't mean that my powers can't accidentally harm someone else." Turning my hands over, my eyes lingered on a section of raw skin that peered out from beneath the sagging bandages. "And it would be a lot worse than a few burns."

"But we'd already spent some time together before. We even held hands, and you didn't seem worried about that. Why did it suddenly bother you that night?"

"My necklace."

"Huh? What necklace?"

"The pale blue one I always wore," I clarified, my hand subconsciously drifting to my bare neck. "It was a kedja."

There was a sharp intake of breath across from me.

"Katya, are you crazy? Why would you wear one of those? It could kill you!"

"It wasn't exactly my idea to wear it," I shrugged. "My

parents gave it to me when I was ten."

"*What?*" Matteo gasped, the single word tinted with equal parts horror and shock. "A kedja is meant to subdue Vaettir prisoners by trapping their powers inside their bodies. Why, in the name of all the Norns, would they subject you to that?"

"Because they thought I *should* be a prisoner."

"What?" Matteo's voice was dark. A spark of genuine anger kindled in his eyes, the flaming heat a stunning contrast to the usual temperate warmth smoldering in the chocolate depths.

Pressing my lips together, I lowered my gaze. Revealing this part of my past to Matteo felt like signing my own death warrant. Still, he deserved to know. He deserved the truth.

So, taking a deep breath, I said tensely, "There was... an accident."

The kitchen was suffocating in its stillness. My heart pounded loudly against my breastbone.

"What happened?" Matteo probed with a gentleness that tugged at my heart. Idly turning the cup around in my hands, I opened the door in my mind to a memory I had long since locked away.

"I had a sister, once," I began. "Madeleine. I called her 'Del' for short. She was eight years older than me, but that didn't stop us from being best friends. We did everything together.

"She was a Daski, too. She taught me everything about my powers—what they are, how they work, how to use them. She was so skilled with her magic. I wanted to be just like her, even though I knew I'd never be able to hold a candle to her. The only way I could ever hold my own against her was by creating ice shields. They came easily to me—like second nature. And they were strong. No one could break them." There was a hint of pride in my voice.

"Del was proud of me. And I, of course, admired her. She was my big sister. I thought we'd always be close. I thought nothing could ever come between us." I paused, swirling the tea in my cup. "But then, one day, a new girl moved in next door. Her name was Rebecca. She was a witch, who specialized in dark magic.

"I think she was in one of Del's classes at school. They became friends almost instantly, and Del started hanging out with her all the time. She introduced Del to dark magic. That was when I started to lose my sister.

"You see, Del was always very ambitious, and dark magic gave her the power she craved. She was hooked on it. That's when I noticed that Del was changing. She was rarely ever home, she stopped spending time with our family, and she started pushing me out of her life.

"One day, in a desperate attempt to spend time with her, I begged her to take me to the park near our house. I guess she was having a good day, because she agreed. She promised me that as soon as she got out of school, we'd go to the park. I ran all the way home from school that day— I was so excited.

"But then, she didn't come home. I waited and waited, but she never showed. When she finally got back later that night, she told my parents that she had gone to Rebecca's house instead. She didn't even bother telling *me* about it. I was so hurt. So, the next day, I confronted her about it. All she could say to me was that I was neither old enough nor interesting enough for her to hang out with. To her, I was nothing more than an annoying little sister. I got so angry.

And... I pushed her. The next thing I knew, there was a dagger of ice flying towards my head.

"I didn't even think before throwing up an ice shield to protect myself. Del's dagger hit it and bounced off, ricocheting back at her. She dove out of the way, but it clipped her shoulder, leaving her with a nasty cut and a few bruises. Later that night, she told our parents that I had attacked her unprovoked. They believed her—they didn't even want to hear my side of the story." I shook my head sadly. "It seems like they never did."

"Why not?"

"I don't know. They just never liked me much, that's all." I gave a half-hearted shrug. "I was an accident. They never planned on having another child after Del. Both my parents were Daskis, and they knew having a Daski child was risky. There's always a fifty percent chance it will turn out evil. But they figured they could prevent that. So, from the moment she was born, they lavished her with everything—love, support, kindness—just to prevent her from becoming one of the 'bad' Daskis.

"As Del grew up, they thought their efforts had been successful. Del was the perfect child—sweet, caring, polite. Still, she was supposed to be their one and only. It was too risky to try for another child. No Daski family has ever had more than one 'good' child. It's almost like there's a quota—no matter how many children you have, one will turn out to be a respectable Daski, while the rest become the villains that you read about in all the legends.

"Anyway, needless to say, my parents weren't thrilled when they had me. They were terrified of me. Oh, they still did their best to treat me like they did Del, in the hopes that I might not turn out 'all that bad,' as they put it. But even before I was born, they had given up on me. And all throughout my childhood, it showed. Any mistake I made was immediately thought to be a sign that I was evil.

"Needless to say, when Del went to them accusing me of attacking her, they were horrified. Their worst fears were confirmed. That's when they gave me the kedja. They forbade me from ever taking it off—from ever using my powers again. In their eyes, it was the only way—short of imprisoning me—to stop me from hurting people and becoming the monster they always feared I'd be." I ran a finger over a grain of wood in the table. "I was ten at the time. I believed them.

"My sister turned eighteen shortly after that, and she left home almost immediately." I swallowed, my throat constricting. "She died a few months later. My parents blamed me for it—and, in a way, I guess I did, too." I shook my head against the memories. "Anyway, they never forgave me, and reminded me of it constantly. That's why I don't really have a relationship with them anymore. It's also why I moved halfway around the world when I got the chance. But even after I left home, I kept the kedja on. I was too afraid of what would happen if I took it off. It wasn't all bad—it let me live a relatively normal life. But the Onemdi kind of put an end to that. The one that was choking me? It tore the kedja off when you shot it with that fireball.

"That's why I didn't want you touching me that night on Torcello. It's why I pushed you away, why I rejected our bond. My magic hasn't had any freedom in fifteen years. Now there's nothing restricting it at all, other than my own willpower. I don't know what to expect from it. I mean, just the other night, I accidentally froze a book I was reading because I was upset. Who's to say my powers wouldn't have a similar effect on a person?" My shoulders sagged despondently. "It just felt safer to keep you, and everyone else, at a distance. This way, I couldn't hurt any of you."

Finished with my story, I kept my eyes carefully affixed to the cup in my hands, refusing to look at Matteo. I was too afraid of what I'd see written across the lines of his face. The ball was in his court now, and while I waited for his reaction, my tea was definitely a much safer focal point for my attention—even with the tiny crystals of ice that were creeping along the rim of the cup and reaching for the surface of its contents. I could only stare at the thin layer of frost numbly.

Suddenly, my field of vision was disrupted by a finger from the other side of the table. I watched curiously as it landed on my teacup, the tip of it a pale orange. Slowly, the ice began to melt, and the cup gradually grew warmer in my hands. Then, its task complete, the digit retreated, and I finally mustered up the courage to glance at its owner.

What I saw on Matteo's face stunned me. There was no judgment, no disgust, no hatred—nothing I had been anticipating. Instead, there was only sympathy, concern, and understanding. And although his eyes held mine in an achingly tender gaze, they still smoldered with rage—a rage that was not directed *at* me but was instead burning *for* me.

"I'm so sorry, Katya," he whispered in a pained voice.

"Thank you," I replied with a small smile. "But it was a long time ago—fifteen years now, actually."

"Time is no factor where pain is concerned." He stared

at me with earnestness, as though granting me permission to acknowledge the grief I had forbidden myself from feeling for nearly two decades.

"You won't hurt me, you know," he stated without so much as a hint of doubt.

"You don't know that," I muttered miserably.

"Yes, I do."

"How?"

Matteo leaned forward, his elbows resting on the table. But instead of answering my question, he responded with one of his own. "Do you think *I* would ever hurt *you*?"

"What?" I was utterly lost now.

"Do you think I would hurt you?" he repeated patiently.

"No! Of course not."

"Why not?"

"Because you're a good person," I answered automatically. "You're kind, patient, warm-hearted. You're like sunshine personified." I blushed, ducking my head as soon as I realized what I had said. "Plus, you clearly have a firm grasp over your powers, and would never use them to hurt someone else."

"Exactly," Matteo stated with a smile.

"Huh?"

"Everything you just said... well, it was very kind. But I could say all of the same things about you. You have a beautiful heart and a beautiful soul. You do not have a heart of ice, you are not cold-blooded, and you most certainly are not a monster. The fact that you're so afraid of hurting others should be proof enough of that. And if you need additional evidence... just look at what happened during the battle on Torcello. You saved my life."

"That was an accident." Then, realizing how that sounded, my eyes widened. "No, that's not what I meant. Saving you wasn't an accident—I meant to do *that*. The ice was the accident."

"It's alright," Matteo chuckled in amusement, raising a hand. "I understand."

I breathed a sigh of relief.

"Don't you see, Katya? You conjured ice to protect me. You didn't even attack the enemy with it, you just stopped the fire from hitting me. In the middle of a battle. That takes a lot of control—and it also shows that you have no malicious intent in your heart."

"What about Del? I didn't mean to hurt her—but I still did."

"Accidents happen," he shrugged. "Just look at your hands. I burned you... hurt you." His voice was strained, and I suddenly realized that he also felt guilty for what his powers had done. "I didn't mean to, but I did. We are Vaettir, after all—things like that are going to happen. But that doesn't make us bad people. It's only in *choosing* to do wrong that we become evil."

"That's what Janara told me."

"She did?"

"Yeah. She also told me that I need to embrace my powers in order to rid myself of my fear of them."

"Well, she's wise beyond her years." He paused. "You have nothing to fear from yourself or your powers."

"How can you know that?"

"I just do. You're not like most other Daskis." Tapping the soulbond on his wrist, he added, "I can feel it." Then, peering closely at me, he said sadly, "You look in the mirror, and you see a monster. But that's not what I see."

"Oh yeah? What do you see, then?"

He gave me the sweetest, most affectionate smile, and my heart skipped a beat. Staring deep into my eyes, he answered honestly, "I see a beautiful woman—on the outside, yes, of course; but, more importantly, on the inside. From the moment I met you, I could sense all of the kindness, the gentleness, the warmth radiating from your heart. It was breathtaking. But the more time I've spent with you, the more our bond has grown, allowing me to see your soul more clearly than ever before. And what I see is more stunning than any words could possibly describe.

"You ask me what I see in you... Well, I see someone with a huge heart, filled with more love, selflessness, and compassion than anyone I've ever known. I see someone with a brilliant mind and a marvelous sense of humor. I see someone with a passionate and honest soul.

"When I look at you, I see someone who is quiet and reserved. Someone who lives in fear of herself because of the lies that she was told all her life, and the abuses that she suffered at the hands of those who were supposed to love her. But, I also see someone who is far stronger and braver than she even knows. Someone who has gracefully handled all of life's challenges, using them to learn and grow rather than allowing them to turn her cold and bitter.

"And, although you may disagree with me on this one, I see someone with special powers. Not only are they rare and unique by nature, but I also happen to think that they're pretty cool." He smirked. "No pun intended.

"Katya, you are the most beautiful, intelligent, intriguing person I have ever met in my life. It is a privilege and an honor just to know you. The fact that fate has chosen *me* as your soulmate is something I still struggle to believe is real. I am so lucky—and so incredibly *grateful*—to be granted that role in your life."

Matteo's feelings flooded our bond, and the combined strength and sincerity of them was overwhelming. A new set of tears sprang unbidden to my eyes as his emotions coursed through me, seeking out and mending every wound in my soul.

"For all of your life, your parents, society—they told you that you were a monster. And, understandably, you believed them, since no one had ever told you any differently. But it's *my* goal to spend the rest of my life proving to you that you're not any of the things they said you are. Regardless of whether or not you want me as your soulmate, as a friend, as nothing at all... I will find a way to ensure that you never again have to fight your demons alone."

In my mind, it was like the clouds had just parted to reveal the brilliant sun beneath them. Matteo's words had struck a chord with me. No matter how many times Nina had insisted that my powers were not a malevolent force, no matter how powerful Janara's own attestations to my morality had been earlier that day, they didn't reach me in quite the same way that Matteo's words just had.

Maybe it was because we were soulmates. Perhaps it was the look of sheer adoration that I saw shining brightly in his eyes. Or, it might have been the trust, acceptance, and affection that I felt radiating through our bond. But, whatever it was, I suddenly felt as though I was seeing the world—and myself—in an entirely different light.

"I still want you as my soulmate, Matteo," I admitted

quietly. "I always did. I'm so sorry that I hurt you, and if you no longer want me—"

I didn't get a chance to finish, because Matteo interrupted softly, but passionately, "Of course, I still want you. I always will."

"But I was *horrible* to you—"

"Shh, va bene. I understand why you said and did those things. All is forgiven." I must have still looked distressed because he added once more with quiet conviction, "Katya, it's okay."

I swallowed, nodding. A stray tear leaked from the corner of my eye, trailing a wet path down my cheek.

"Katya—"

"Kat," I interrupted.

"What?"

"Everyone close to me calls me Kat."

Judging by the small smile that appeared on Matteo's lips, he understood what I was trying to say.

"Ok," he nodded. "Kat."

I gave him a watery smile. Then, resting my hand beside Matteo's, I pulled the sleeve back from my left wrist to reveal the braid encircling it. Seeing the marks—which were now a bit bolder in color, but still rather pale—side-by-side for the first time sent a ripple of happiness through me.

"I really want to try this—*us*," I declared. "It may not be easy—"

"Love never is," Matteo retorted kindly. And if I forgot to breathe when he mentioned the word "love," who was to know? "But the Norns wouldn't have bound us together if there wasn't a way for us to make it work."

Matteo lifted his hand from the table, extending it

towards me, palm outstretched. My gray eyes sought out his chocolate ones, finding nothing but warmth, joy, and love—yes, *love*—dancing within them. His entire demeanor exuded positivity. And it was infectious—spreading through my veins and warming me from the inside out.

Biting my lip, I extended my hand slowly toward his, determined not to hurt him. The distance narrowed, the gap between us closing. My hand hovered over his. Then, with one final encouraging nod from Matteo, I gently lowered my hand to his.

At first, I touched only a single finger to his skin. Holding my breath, I waited for something to happen. When nothing did, a sigh of relief gusted from my lips. Feeling emboldened, I allowed another finger to linger against his hand. Still, nothing happened. So, with Matteo watching patiently, I continued to connect our hands one finger at a time, until our palms were finally resting flush against each other.

The moment our hands connected, a warm tingle like an electric shock raced up my arm, spreading throughout my body. I noticed that Matteo's skin felt warm against mine, but not uncomfortably so. It was more like the rays of the sun on a cold winter day—gentle and comforting.

Then, there was something else—faint at first, but then stronger. It was a feeling of awe, trust, overwhelming joy. Initially, I thought they were my own emotions. But there was a duality to them—a simultaneous, yet parallel, rush of those sentiments through my body—and I knew they did not belong solely to me.

My eyes flickered up to Matteo's. From that single look, I could tell that he could feel my innermost emotions, just as I could his. Likewise, I knew he must be experiencing the same tingling in our soulbond—a pulsating current, as though the connection between us was revitalizing itself. It was a marvelous sensation—our souls recognizing each other, embracing each other, and finally merging together as one.

I gazed in wonder at our joined hands, our soulmarks almost luminous on our wrists. Matteo smiled, mirroring my own huge grin. Shifting our hands slightly, he intertwined our fingers.

"I think we can make this work," I whispered. And with the way that Matteo beamed in response, I was certain that he could have outshone the sun itself.

CHAPTER THIRTEEN

I didn't know how long Matteo and I sat there, our hands joined, simply enjoying the feel of our bond as it shimmered and danced in our souls. It was like finding the missing piece to a puzzle.

Matteo's thumb was rubbing soothing circles against the back of my hand, over a part of my skin that wasn't burned.

"How are your hands?" he asked.

"They're alright," I replied, albeit a little too quickly. Matteo raised a skeptical eyebrow at me.

"Well, they might hurt a little bit," I amended with a blush.

"May I take a look?"

I nodded, allowing him to cradle my hands in his own as he inspected them closely. The longer he peered at the various burns and slack bandages, the more his frown deepened. When he finally finished with his examination, he hummed in disapproval.

"This wrapping needs to be redone," he commented. "And some more burn salve should be applied. Disinfecting these burns again couldn't hurt, either."

"I did the best I could," I murmured. "It's a bit hard with only one hand." At Matteo's questioning look, I added guiltily, "I wouldn't let Nina or Janara help me—you know, because of the whole Daski thing..."

Matteo said nothing, though I caught the quick look of understanding that flashed across his face.

"Well, then I'll just have to remedy that, won't I?"

"Matteo, you don't have to—"

"I know I don't have to," he interrupted softly, already standing to retrieve the necessary supplies. "But, I want to."

There was a beseeching expression in his eyes that made my heart clench. I knew I wouldn't be able to deny him this—not this time. Truth be told, I didn't want to.

"Alright," I conceded. "Thank you."

Matteo smiled. "I'll be right back."

When he returned a couple of minutes later, there was a first aid kit in his hands. Placing it on the table, he sank back down into the seat across from me, setting to work without a moment's hesitation.

I observed him intently as he treated my injuries. He kept his face carefully blank, but every now and then, while cleaning a particularly nasty burn, something akin to guilt ghosted across his face. Concern always replaced it immediately, before his features were once again schooled into an unreadable mask.

Despite the shifting emotions on Matteo's face, his hands were steady. Gentle yet sure, they dabbed disinfectant onto my burns, applied salve to the raw skin, and wrapped my hands securely in clean bandages. Tears burned behind my eyes at the sheer amount of tender affection with which Matteo was treating me. Never before had I been on the receiving end of such a blatant show of love. I swallowed thickly against the emotions choking me.

"There," Matteo announced proudly as he tied a knot in the last strip of gauze enveloping my palm. "All done."

"Grazie," I whispered in awe, studying Matteo's handiwork. "This is much better than anything I could have done."

"All of the credit goes to my mother," he replied with a small smile as he packed the medical supplies back into the tiny kit. "She's a doctor."

"Really?"

"Sì. She tried to teach me and Leo, but I was the only one that had the attention span for it. I've learned a lot from her over the years. Actually, as a child, I wanted to be a doctor, too."

"Why didn't you?"

He shrugged. "I realized that I only wanted to be a doctor because my mom was one. Although I had a talent for it, my true passion has always been music. So, I became a musician instead."

"My parents would've been furious if I ever made a decision like that."

"Well, your parents aren't exactly what I'd call exemplary," he countered with a trace of bitterness. "But yes, I was very fortunate to have parents who supported my dreams."

"How did you discover your love for music?"

"My grandfather was a pianist. I grew up listening to him play. I think he started teaching *me* to play before I could even walk." He chuckled fondly at the memory. "We would spend hours together each week, playing the piano and singing. He's the reason I fell in love with all the greats—Caruso, Bocelli, Pavarotti. My favorite, though, has always been Plácido Domingo."

"Your grandfather had good taste in music."

"The best," he replied with a smile. "And he could hold his own among any of them—he was a fantastic singer. He used to sing in our church choir. I wanted to be just like him and become a singer myself."

"Why didn't you?"

"I didn't possess the same talent for singing that he did. I'm much better at writing and playing music."

"Wait—you write music, too?"

"I dabble at it. My dream is to one day compose music professionally. But, it's a difficult field to break into—and my music never quite seems to be ready."

"I'm sure it's better than you think it is," I said encouragingly. "You should put something out there—everyone will love it."

"You haven't even heard my music," Matteo retorted mildly.

"No, but music comes from the soul, so any song written by you is bound to be beautiful."

Matteo's eyes glimmered with emotion. "Would you like to hear one?"

"Absolutely!"

"Come with me," he said, taking my hand and tugging me from my chair. He led me into the den, and over to the piano nestled in the far corner. With a reassuring squeeze to my hand, he pulled me down beside him on the bench.

Clearing his throat nervously, his fingers skimmed lightly over the ivory keys.

"I wrote this song about you," he confessed. Then, taking a deep breath, he started to play. His fingers moved nimbly and confidently over the keys. The notes blended together flawlessly, filling the otherwise empty apartment with a melody that was heart-wrenching in its beauty. Cheery, yet tinged with melancholy, the tune rose and fell as gently as the wind. Listening to it felt like standing in the middle of a snow-covered forest, shrouded in peace, with only the memories and sentimentality brought about by solitude as company.

I stared at Matteo, mesmerized by the way his entire being was transported by the music he was creating. His eyes were closed as he allowed the melody to carry him away. His face was a canvas of passionate emotion, each note painting a new hue across his features.

I got so lost in the moment and the music, that I didn't even notice when the song ended. Even after Matteo had stopped playing, it was like I could still hear it in my mind, my heart tapping out a rhythmic staccato as my soul floated into that dreamy void only accessible on the wings of a ballad. It was only the feel of a gentle hand cupping my face that drew me back into the stillness of the present.

Matteo swiped away a tear that had escaped my eye and was trailing slowly down my cheek.

"I should probably rethink my career if my music makes people cry," he murmured teasingly. Yet I detected the hint of worry lying just beneath the surface of his words.

"No," I said, laying one of my own hands atop his. "That was beautiful, Matteo. I've never heard anything like it."

"You liked it?"

"*Liked* it? I *loved* it," I responded ardently, giving his fingers a squeeze. "Thank you for sharing that with me."

He brushed his thumb over my cheek once more, staring into my eyes with gratitude and adoration. I had no idea how long we stayed like that—maybe a few seconds, maybe an eternity. But the next thing I knew, he started to lean closer. I held my breath as the distance between us narrowed...

And my eyes fluttered closed just as his lips touched mine.

The kiss was tender and chaste, yet full of passionate feeling. And with that kiss, the final barriers around my heart collapsed. I felt inundated with warmth and light—as though somewhere within me, a bright sun had just dawned over a dark horizon. And although there weren't sparks or fireworks like typical romance stories would have you believe, this gradual, subtle incandescence was far better.

After a few moments, Matteo broke the kiss, pulling back only far enough to press our foreheads together. Blinking up at him, I grinned broadly. From behind his glasses, his own jubilant eyes sparkled. With fingers that barely touched my skin, he brushed a few strands of hair away from my face, tucking them behind my ear. My eyes flickered closed.

It was pure perfection, being close to Matteo like this. In my contentment, my mind was blissfully blank. My heart felt like it was bursting with happiness. Everything in the world, in that moment, felt *right*.

And on my left wrist, my soulmark thrummed merrily, as though celebrating our bond's victory over my darker demons.

CHAPTER FOURTEEN

The next few days passed uneventfully enough. Thankfully, ever since that night in Torcello, there hadn't been a single sign of the Devil or the Onemdi. His promise to return on the 24th appeared to be genuine and, barring any other attempts to summon him, he would not reappear a moment sooner. It was odd that such an evil creature was so adamant about staying true to his word.

For what it was worth, the people of Venice were also keeping a low profile. Whether that was because they had learned their lesson from the shopkeeper and his son, or because they didn't have any other tricks up their sleeves, was up for debate. Either way, we were grateful that we hadn't heard of any other attempts to summon the Devil.

Unfortunately, there was also no word from Nina or Leo. It was as though they had both been plucked from the

Earth. Only my nearly decade-long friendship with Nina, and Matteo's lifetime as Leo's brother, kept us from thinking that they had completely abandoned us to our own devices.

As though trying to make up for the absence, Janara and Arun were around *constantly*. They seemed to feel responsible for keeping an eye on us in the absence of our siblings—or, in my case, surrogate sibling. Janara was my stealthy, subtle shadow; and Arun was Matteo's much louder and conspicuous one. Much of the time though, we didn't even notice their watchful presence since we were usually doing research with them anyway. Together, we spent hours upon endless hours bent over books, hunched at computers, browsing on our phones for any potential solution to the "Devil problem," as Arun liked to call it. Then, we would spend what felt like ages talking through and hashing out each individual theory, crossing them off our list of possible options before once again starting at square one.

Which is why we were all currently huddled around the kitchen table in Matteo's apartment while the world around us was fast asleep—me with my head in my hands, Matteo with a cup of tea in his, and Janara and Arun poised as though ready to hurl themselves at each other across the wooden surface.

"I know it's not ideal, but it's our only option!"

"It's suicide!"

"We don't have another choice!"

"There's always another choice!"

"We've been through all the other options. There's no other way."

"Oh, well that's just bloody brilliant," Arun scoffed. "A

force of four Vaettir against an entire *army* of demons led by the Devil himself!"

"Arun—"

"No, Janara. Do you even hear yourself? Your plan is pure insanity!"

"Well, we have to get Aella back somehow!"

"By getting ourselves killed?!"

"Would you rather our sister be killed?!"

"Of course not! But what good is it to save her if we all end up dead in the process? Who's going to be there to protect her from the Devil once we're gone? And even if she somehow survives *without* the Devil getting her... what's to become of her? In case you've forgotten, we don't have any other family. *We're all we have, Janara.*"

"You think I don't know that?" she hissed. "You think I haven't thought about what might happen? But we don't exactly have a lot of options right now, Arun! I'm just trying to do whatever I can to get out sister back alive."

Arun deflated slightly at that. "I know, I know," he muttered, running a frustrated hand through his short hair.

"Not to be the bearer of bad news," Matteo cut in. "But we can't forget about Venezia, either. We need to protect the people here, too. And if we do a frontal attack against the Devil and his army, only to get ourselves killed in the process, then there would be no one left to defend the city."

"So, we should just forget about our sister?" Janara quipped sardonically.

"No, not at all," Matteo hurried to assuage her. "I'm just saying that we have more than one objective. There are a lot of people who are counting on us."

"Matteo's right," I said quickly. "Somehow, we need to do both things—get Aella back safely *and* protect Venice from the Devil and the Onemdi."

"Then we're going to need back-up, and lots of it," Arun commented matter-of-factly. "Why don't we scour the streets of Venice—try to find people to help us? I mean, there might not be any other Kongeligs or Daskis around, since we're rare breeds. But there have got to be a few Voktere who will help us."

"Leo and I thought of that," Matteo said. "In those few days after the second attack on Torcello, we tried finding some Voktere who would be willing to help us... but all of the ones we met refused to have anything to do with us."

"But their city could be destroyed!"

"Right now, that's only a potential possibility. It's not a reality for them—not yet. Many of them hope to escape the Devil's fury one way or another. But, if they join forces with us, it's the same as signing a death warrant for themselves and their families. That's not a risk they're willing to take."

"So, we're on our own," Janara uttered darkly.

"Well, if we're going to be alone in this, then we don't have the strength of numbers on our side. Hmm." Arun tapped his chin in thought. "What about a time machine?"

We all pinned Arun with equally incredulous—if somewhat exasperated—looks.

"You *are* joking," Janara deadpanned. "A time machine? *That's* your solution?"

"Well, yeah," Arun shrugged. "We could go back to the Austrian invasion and stop the woman's deal with the Devil from happening."

"And disrupt the entire flow of time in the process!"

Janara puffed out a long, low breath, calming herself. "Arun, unless you know something I don't, time machines don't exist—and I highly doubt that any of us in this room are qualified to build one. Even if we could, you can't go messing with time. Changing the past also changes the present and the future. To change something that happened that long ago... you could end up altering the entire course of history."

"Oh," Arun mumbled, rubbing his neck sheepishly. "I didn't think about that."

"What if we don't alter the past, but recreate it?" I asked. All eyes turned to me.

"Not you, too," Janara groaned, burying her face in her hands.

"Janara, wait. Kat," Matteo turned to me. "What do you mean?"

"Well, a witch helped make the contract between the woman and the Devil two centuries ago... so why can't *we* find a different witch to help us either rewrite or invalidate the contract?"

Silence descended over the kitchen as my three compatriots pondered the suggestion. Had the stakes of our conversation not been so high, it would have been comical to watch their faces almost simultaneously shift from thoughtful seriousness to cautious hopefulness before morphing into excited optimism.

"That might just work," Janara murmured, her eyes nearly translucent as they glittered brightly. I could see the wheels churning furiously in her mind.

"Of course it will!" Arun replied eagerly.

"Hold on," Matteo interrupted, holding up a hand. "It's not quite that simple. These days, witches are even rarer than Kongeligs or Daskis. Even back in the eighteenth century, when the woman first summoned the Devil here, witches were scarce and rapidly dying out—an unfortunate result of the witch trials in the previous centuries. They're virtually extinct now, and those that do remain hide their identities out of fear of persecution. I doubt we'd be able to find a witch, let alone one who would admit to being one. And even if we could, they probably wouldn't be willing to help us."

"Matteo's right," Janara sighed, her face falling. "It was a great idea, Kat, but our chances of finding a witch to help us is next to none."

"Then I guess that brings us back to square one."

"Yeah—a frontal attack." Arun turned an imploring gaze upon his sister. "There's really no other way?"

"Not that I can see," she answered regretfully.

"Matteo?" he probed desperately. Matteo only shook his head helplessly, giving the blonde an apologetic look.

"Kat? You have to have another idea," Arun all but pleaded.

"I'm sorry, Arun, but I don't," I replied sadly. "Believe me, I wish I did. But we've been through every possible course of action the past few weeks, to no avail. Your sister's right—attacking the Onemdi when they come back to Venezia is the only hope we have."

Arun audibly gulped. Janara eyed him with concern as she waited for his reaction. He was frozen in place, staring blankly at the wall for several long minutes. The occasional blinking of his eyes was the only evidence we had that he hadn't turned to stone. We waited. And waited. And waited. Exchanging nervous glances with Janara and Matteo, I vaguely wondered if we had permanently broken Arun.

Finally, with a small shake of his head, Arun broke out of his daze. He looked first at Matteo, then at me, before his eyes fell upon his sister. For a few seconds, they stared at each other, sharing a silent conversation. Then, with a definitive nod of his head and a tired sigh, Arun stated, "Well, I guess if we're going to die, then we may as well go down swinging."

"That's the spirit!" Janara exclaimed with forced enthusiasm, clapping him on the shoulder. He snorted humorlessly, leaning back against the counter and crossing his arms over his chest. "Now, we're going to want to try to survive this fight at all costs—"

"You've got that right," Arun sniped.

"Which means we're going to have to start planning. We all need to prepare." Janara pointed at me and Matteo. "You two are going to have to train to make sure your powers—and your control over them—are in top shape. You and I—" she continued, jabbing her thumb at Arun and herself, respectively. "Are going to have to stock up on arrows and do some target practice."

"Right," Arun nodded.

"We're also going to need..."

Janara's voice faded into the background of my consciousness. It was shrouded by the weight and reality of the situation, which had suddenly settled heavily upon my shoulders.

Something Arun said had just struck me. We were going to die.

Of course, it wasn't certain by any means, but the odds were definitely against us.

It was fitting, really, that after losing my sister as a result—albeit an indirect one—of my powers, that I would face my own demise using them to save someone else's sister... not to mention an entire city.

A warm hand covered mine, and I knew who it belonged to without needing to look.

Matteo, who was watching me with more concern than I had ever received.

Matteo, who was the embodiment of everything good and light about the world.

Matteo, who might die in three days' time.

The mere thought of it made my heart constrict painfully. Knowing that I could die was terrifying. But the thought of a world without Matteo in it was unbearable. And in that moment, I knew that I would do anything and everything to prevent that from happening. So long as I had a breath left in my body, I would protect him at all costs.

If I was successful, he would survive to see the dawn of Christmas Day—and many more Christmas Days to come. Of course, with my death, he would have to live with a broken soulbond, which I'd heard is excruciating—most unlucky individuals who had experienced it likened it to having a scalding knife sliced through their souls, cutting and severing their very cores until there was nothing left but burning, frayed remains and a gaping hole where their soulmate's essence had once been. It would be a horrible fate for Matteo to endure, but it was better than him facing a premature death.

Something warm and gentle swirled through me, shaking me from my thoughts.

"Kat? Are you back with me?"

I blinked at Matteo a few times, confused by the question.

"Huh?"

"I was talking to you, but you weren't answering. It was like you were in some sort of trance."

"Oh," I said dumbly. I hadn't realized I had zoned out. "Sorry."

"You don't need to apologize—I was just worried," he replied, his face losing a few of the worry lines that creased it. "You were thinking pretty hard."

"Yeah, I guess I was," I answered with a small smile. Then, noticing the quietness of the kitchen, I asked, "Where are Janara and Arun?"

"They left a few minutes ago," Matteo responded, frowning. "Are you sure you're alright?"

"I'm fine."

He sighed tiredly. "Kat, I know you've spent your life on your own, hiding your true feelings the way everyone told you that you should. But you don't have to hide from me... not ever."

"I know that now," I confirmed softly. I turned my hand so I could link my fingers with his. Worrying my bottom lip between my teeth, I observed our joined hands with a bittersweet fondness. "I was just thinking about the twenty-fourth—about what's going to happen."

"Me, too," he confessed quietly. Giving my hand a squeeze, he murmured firmly, "I won't let anything happen to you."

"And *I* won't let anything happen to *you*," I stated fiercely. An affectionate look crossed Matteo's face. It flickered briefly to sadness, then settled on determination.

"Well, then, it seems that the Devil will be up against quite the formidable force."

"Indeed, he will."

Sitting in the quiet kitchen, our hands linked, we relished in our closeness. Then, suddenly, Matteo declared, "We're going out."

"What?"

"On a date," he clarified. "I think we could both use a distraction from everything that's going on. Besides, our last date was rudely interrupted by an army of demons—I think we deserve another one."

"I would say so," I grinned. Then, in a soft voice, I added, "A date sounds wonderful."

"Excellent!" He stood, pulling me up with him. "Andiamo, *amore mio*."

I blushed as he raised my hand and placed a tender kiss on the back of it, then happily followed him as he tugged me out the door.

CHAPTER FIFTEEN

We didn't go to Torcello for our date this time. We had learned that lesson well the first time around. Instead, Matteo and I spent our second date confined to Murano. We ate dinner at a quaint restaurant, enjoyed some gelato while walking around Campo Santo Stefano, and simply relished in each other's company as we wandered hand-in-hand through the narrow alleys, talking about nothing in particular. Matteo even treated me to a gondola ride—an extravagance in which I had only indulged once when I first came to Venice. It was far too expensive to take repeated rides in the small vessels.

It was a perfect evening. But then, any time spent with Matteo was perfect. It was like going home. Or, at least, what I always imagined a true home to be—a place where I felt comfortable and safe, surrounded by those who loved and accepted me for who I was. There was no pressure to be perfect, no need to change myself to fit his expectations. It was understood that I could—and should—be unashamedly, unabashedly myself. And every time I laughed so much that a snort would escape, every time I rambled a bit too much about some topic in history that almost no one else in the world would care about, every time I was distracted by a picturesque view or a beautiful song or the feel of the wind on my face and would stop to appreciate it, something warm and fond rushed through our bond. It was like being hugged from the inside. Then I would look at Matteo, finding an expression of aching softness, quiet awe, and deep love that both reassured and encouraged me. In short, it was freeing to be with Matteo, and I vaguely wondered if this was what it felt like to fly. My soul, after all, was soaring.

As we stepped out of the gondola, Matteo held my hand to help me out of the boat. My foot had just touched solid ground when my phone started to ring. Murmuring a quick apology to Matteo, I pulled the small device from my pocket, glancing at the display. My brow furrowed in confusion, and an uneasy feeling settled in the pit of my stomach.

"Janara?"

"Kat, we have trouble."

"What do you mean?" I asked, casting a worried look at Matteo. He instinctively moved a step closer to me, face creasing in concern.

"It seems some of the less humane of Venice's citizens have decided that they'd rather lose a few kids than their city," she answered scornfully. "I heard a group of the so-called city elders talking. Their decision was, and I quote,

'Sacrifice the few to save the whole.' Tomorrow, when the school holiday starts, they're going to choose six kids at random and bring them to the Devil to fulfill the contract."

"What?!" I gasped. "They can't do that!"

"Which is why we need to move tonight," Janara continued grimly.

"We'll—" I suddenly froze, something about Janara's previous statement making me unsettled. "Wait, six kids? But the Devil asked for seven..."

There was a pregnant pause on the other end of the line that made my heart clench.

"Janara?"

"They're going to count the child the Devil already took as number seven."

"Aella," I breathed, horrified.

"Yes," came the terse answer. Then, a shuffling sound emanated from the speaker. "The elders have forced our hand. We're out of time to plan or prepare. The four of us will just have to do the best with what we have. I'm on my way to Torcello right now. Arun is with me. We'll meet you there."

"Right. Matteo and I will be there as soon as we can," I promised before ending the call.

"What happened?" Matteo inquired quietly. I stared up at him, trying to speak past the shock clouding my mind.

"Some of Venice's elders decided that the city was worth more than the lives of seven children. They're going to kidnap six of them tomorrow to bring to the Devil as payment—and they're counting Aella as the seventh soul to sacrifice."

Matteo muttered an explicative. Had the situation been different, I would have been stunned by it—cursing was so uncharacteristic of him. If nothing else, that in itself revealed just how upset he was by this news.

"So, the decision's out of our hands—we fight tonight."

I nodded. "Janara and Arun are on their way to Torcello as we speak."

Dread fleetingly raced through our bond, followed by resignation.

"Then let's go," Matteo said, grabbing my hand as we raced across the island toward the port closest to Torcello.

We got to the docking point just as the last vaporetto was departing.

"No!" I shouted, watching as the vessel zipped away into the open waters of the Adriatic.

"We have to find another way across. Maybe there's someone who would be willing to take us—"

"Need a ride?" came a familiar voice from behind us. Matteo and I spun around, mirrored looks of disbelief and shock on our faces.

"Nina?" I breathed. "Leo?"

"Ciao," Nina greeted almost cautiously, fidgeting with her fingers in a way that I had long ago come to associate solely with her. Leo, surprisingly, remained silent, but he did give a small, sheepish wave.

"Where were you two?" Matteo questioned, his tone caught somewhere between relief and anger. His face, however, was thunderous, and Nina and Leo both hesitated, casting nervous glances at each other.

"We were looking for someone," Nina explained quickly, being the first one to recover from Matteo's intense, heated scrutiny. That was yet another surprise.

"Yeah, someone who could help us save Venezia," Leo jumped in. Matteo blinked several times, then sighed heavily, pinching the bridge of his nose.

"Alright, explain."

"Well, it was Nina's idea, really," Leo began, giving her a look full of pride and adoration. I tucked that small detail away in the back of my mind to revisit later—it was significant for reasons I couldn't spend time dwelling on right now. "She thought that since reading books and talking to other Venetians wasn't getting us anywhere, maybe going back to original sources from the time would be of some help. I don't know how she managed it—it was honestly pretty amazing—but she actually tracked down the original contract signed between the woman and the Devil two hundred years ago."

"What?" I was stunned, as well as a bit embarrassed that, as a scholar of history, I hadn't thought of that myself. It simply hadn't occurred to me that the contract might still be out there somewhere—everything that had been happening over the course of the past few weeks felt too much like fantasy to be reality.

Leo pulled a folded piece of parchment from the pocket of his coat, carefully unfolding it to reveal a paragraph of loopy letters scrawled in fading black ink, with two signatures at the bottom—one in a script that would have been elegant if it weren't for the rust-colored liquid in which it was written; the other in sharp, jagged lettering that even now seemed to glow faintly against the yellowed paper. My own words from a couple of weeks ago wafted up from the depths of my mind: *Both the woman and the Devil signed the contract—the woman with her own blood, the Devil with the fires of Hell.*

Seeing the physical evidence of the deal that the woman—according to the contract, her name was Maria Pesaro—made with the Devil somehow made the entire situation all the more real. A cold chill raced through me.

"Once we had the contract and knew the woman's name, we were able to track down some of her descendants. That's where Leo's brilliant people skills came in," Nina continued. "You see, there are other myths and legends about contracts that the Devil has made with people throughout the course of history. In some of them, people found loopholes in their contracts—usually by sacrificing the life of an animal in the stead of a person. Yes, those plans occasionally went awry—such as with the man who built the Rialto bridge—but there were many other attempts at deception that *were* successful. Which got me thinking—if people could replace a human soul with an animal one to trick the Devil, why couldn't we replace one family member with another for that same purpose?"

"I don't follow," I said.

"Our entire problem revolves around this contract," Nina explained, pointing at the document in question. "The Devil came here seeking the payment he was owed according to his agreement with Maria Pesaro. But Maria is dead and has been for over two hundred years. Which leaves us to deal with the repercussions. Right now, our options are to either fulfill the contract or let the Devil lay waste to the city—but we can't sacrifice the children to save Venezia, nor can we sacrifice Venezia to save the children. What we *can* do, however, is undo the contract."

"Eh?" This time it was Matteo who voiced the confusion I was feeling, his face scrunched up as though trying to work out a difficult math problem. All traces of anger had evaporated, replaced only by complete bafflement.

"The validity of a normal contract is usually based on a person's signature—something that is a unique identifying factor only for that person. But this contract is different—it's signed in blood. Therefore, its validity is based on Maria Pesaro's blood. But blood isn't unique to a single person like a signature is... it's shared by direct family members, passed down from one generation to the next. So, if Maria signed this contract, I'm assuming that one of her descendants—in other words, someone who shares her blood—could nullify it."

I processed that for a few moments, hope bubbling up inside of me with each passing second. Everything Nina said made sense. Of course, there was no precedent for any of this, but her reasoning seemed logical. Maybe she was onto something

"So, we went to go find one of her descendants," Leo joined in. "That's why we left. In fact—" he turned, ushering forward a woman who had been standing awkwardly behind him throughout our conversation. "Katya, Matteo—this is Elena Bauer. She's the only living descendant of Maria Pesaro and Franz Bauer."

Elena extended her hand in greeting, smiling sweetly. She was positively stunning, with her alabaster skin, long obsidian hair, and sparkling blue eyes. Tall and slim, she held herself with relaxed elegance. Her Italian and Austrian features were perfectly balanced, and for a moment I had an unsettling feeling that I was currently meeting Maria and Franz first-hand.

"Do you have a plan for how to have her annul the

contract?" Matteo asked.

"We looked into that," Leo responded. "All we have to do is add an addendum to the contract that reverses the original terms, then have Elena sign it."

"In blood," Nina added. Leo nodded.

"What about the Devil? Won't he also have to sign it again?" I questioned.

"Well, yes," Nina said a bit nervously. "But we have a plan for that, too."

"Which is...?"

"This." She held up a small golden key.

"Is that—?"

"Yup," she nodded. "The Key of Time—the same one that the Devil used to bring Franz Bauer back from the dead."

"Our plan is to have Elena use the key—accompanied by one of us—to travel back to when Maria and the Devil originally signed the contract," Leo explained. "We have to get the timing just right—after the Devil has looked over the contract and Maria has signed it, but before the Devil has added his own signature. The idea is that, at that moment, we'll create a distraction. Elena—as Maria's descendant, and therefore the only other person allowed to alter the document—will add the addendum that voids all of the terms of the contract. Then we'll leave before the Devil even notices we're there."

"If all goes as planned, the Devil will sign the contract without noticing the change. And when we arrive back here in the present, the change will be on the contract. Then, all we need to do is have Elena sign the contract while the Devil is still on Torcello. He has to be here, otherwise the document won't recognize Elena's signature as valid. Once it's signed, Leo or I can sign as a witness, and the terms will officially be nullified. At that point, the Devil will no longer have any claim to Venezia or its citizens," Nina finished.

"Why can't we add the addendum before Maria signs it? Wouldn't that be easier?"

Nina shook her head. "It would stop Maria's reunion with Franz, and would essentially change history. That could cause some serious repercussions. We have no choice but to do it this way."

"It's risky," Matteo commented. "There's a lot that could go wrong."

"We know," Leo nodded solemnly. "But it's our best shot."

"And you're alright with this?" I inquired of Elena.

"Oh yes, of course," she answered definitively. I was momentarily distracted by her heavy accent, which was neither Italian nor German. It sounded... *French*? "A little blood is worth saving Venice and its children. Even if nullifying the contract were to cause me harm, I would gladly lay down my life if it meant saving even just the one child who has been kidnapped by the Devil."

"You know about Aella?" I asked, touched by her sentiment.

"Yes, Leo and Nina told me about her when they found me in Colmar."

"Colmar?" That confirmed it. I turned to Nina and Leo. "You went to France?"

"Sì," Leo shrugged. "That's where Elena lives, so that's where we went."

"When they ran away from Venice, Maria and Franz relocated to France. They hoped to settle down together in a small town," Elena explained. "Since France had just come out of the revolution and things were still politically unstable, it was possible for them to... oh, what is the term? Ah, yes—fly under the radar. They ended up in Colmar, which was similar to Venice in so many ways that they simply couldn't resist living there. Our family has stayed in Colmar ever since."

"That's why it was so easy to track her down once we knew where Maria and Franz ended up," Nina commented. "Speaking of tracking people down. Where were you and Matteo off to? We were looking for you two everywhere."

"Torcello," I answered. "A few townspeople decided they were going to kidnap six children tomorrow after the school holiday starts, and offer them to the Devil as a means of fulfilling the contract."

"But the Devil wanted seven souls," Nina stated slowly.

"Yes—they're going to let him keep Aella as the seventh." I ignored Nina's gasp of shock, continuing, "Which means that we only have tonight to make our move. A direct attack was the only thing we could think to do. There were no other options—until now. Janara and Arun are already there. Matteo and I were on our way to meet them, but we just missed the vaporetto. We need to find someone to take us over there."

"No, we don't," Leo said.

"What do you mean, 'we don't'?" Matteo questioned hotly. "We have to get over there to help our friends! We're the only ones who can save Aella and Venezia."

"I mean," Leo interrupted with a raised eyebrow. "That we don't need to find someone to ferry us over. Nina and I can take care of that."

Before Matteo or I could respond, the two of them moved up to the edge of the canal. Nina raised her hands, palms facing the rippling waters of the Adriatic. At first, nothing happened. But then, slowly, the water started vibrating. It trembled and shook, like an earthquake splitting the ground beneath its surface. Nina lowered her head in concentration, sliding her hands in opposite directions. In time with her movements, the water folded over on itself as it gradually began to separate. Soon, the canal had parted in half, the water swirling within itself as it rose into two liquid walls.

Sensing that the timing was right, Leo then extended his own hands, palms facing the sky. As he lifted his hands, the earth at the bottom of the canal rose up, creating a bridge of dirt and stone extending out into the open sea in the direction of Torcello.

"Go," Leo commanded, his eyes never leaving the earth that he was manipulating. A bead of sweat broke out on his brow. "This bridge will take you to Torcello. Take Elena with you. Nina and I will be there shortly."

I was stunned. Parting an ocean, moving the Earth itself—they were no small feats, even for the most skilled Voktere. But there was no time to even be shocked by what Nina and Leo had just managed. So, with a nod and a hasty word of thanks, Matteo and I shepherded Elena onto the earthen passage and hurried toward Torcello.

CHAPTER SIXTEEN

When we arrived on Torcello an hour later, it was eerily silent—as though the island itself knew what was about to happen, and was holding its breath.

"Where is everyone?" I whispered. It felt like speaking too loudly would shatter the world around us. "Why is it so quiet?"

"Something feels wrong about this," Elena commented.

Matteo looked around warily, his face lined with trepidation. Placing a protective hand on my back, he whispered, "Come on, we need to find Janara and Arun."

Together, the three of us crept forward along the brick path in the direction of the campanile, the houses... and the Devil's bridge. Dusk was settling like a purple veil over the land. Shadows stretched across the ground, climbed walls, danced across alleyways. Our footsteps echoed loudly, mingling with the consistent lapping of the water against the walls of the canal beside us. Above, the sky was nearly black, with just a tinge of the blood-red sun still visible on the distant horizon. Other than the millions of stars that were starting to peek out from the dark expanse, there was no one to observe our movements.

So why did it feel like there were eyes watching us everywhere?

Bang!

Matteo, Elena, and I all jumped in unison, spinning around to stare fearfully into the alley directly to our left. Elena slapped a hand across her mouth to stifle the squeak that escaped. An angry hiss emanated from the darkness, followed by an offended *meow*! Then, a black cat darted out of the alley. Startled, I stumbled back a step into Matteo, who steadied me with gentle hands, though the rest of his body had frozen rigidly. My hand instinctively flew out, a small dagger of ice flinging toward the small black blob that my panicked brain had not yet identified as a cat. The feline skittered along the wall, barely visible in the dimming light, hissing and spitting angrily at the ice that shattered against the wall just above its head, before scurrying into another alley a few feet away.

"It was just a cat," I observed, huffing out a breath of relief.

"Let's hope nothing else pops out at us," Matteo said dryly, still glaring at the alley into which the cat had disappeared. "We have enough problems as it is."

"It's good to know you're on your toes, though."

This time, I couldn't stop the scream that burst from my mouth as I swiveled in Matteo's protective embrace to face the source of the new voice. With one eyebrow quirked in mild amusement and her arms crossed loosely across her chest, Janara stood silhouetted against our darkening surroundings. She raised a single placating hand when she spotted the hand that I had unconsciously lifted once more.

"Woah, there, Frosty," she warned. "I'm one of the good guys."

"Sorry," I muttered, lowering my hand and resting it lightly on the arm that Matteo had wrapped around me.

"I'm glad to see that you two made it—I got nervous when I saw that the last scheduled vaporetto for today had arrived here without you."

"We missed it by a matter of seconds," I stated. "But thankfully, Nina and Leo chose that moment to return. They, uh... gave us a lift."

"Where are they?"

"Back on Murano. They had to find a boat to get here. Long story." I waved off the look of confusion she gave me in a clear move that promised *I'll explain later*.

"Alright. Who's she?" Janara nodded in Elena's direction.

"I am Elena Bauer."

"She's the daughter of Maria Pesaro and Franz Bauer—that woman who signed the contract with the Devil and her Austrian lover," Matteo clarified. "That's where Nina and Leo went—to find her. They think she may be able to nullify the contract."

"That would save Aella, the other children, and Venice—and without a fight," Janara noted, her eyes widening.

"Exactly."

"Do you have the contract?"

"Leo does. He should be here with Nina soon," I replied.

"Good. In the meantime, we have to come up with a plan. Even if we undo the contract, it won't change the fact that Aella was taken to Hell by the Devil and the Onemdi. We have to find a way to get her back."

"What are you thinking?" I asked, already able to tell by her voice that she had some sort of strategy laid out in her head.

"Well, our best bet is going to be to split up—divide and conquer. First, Arun and I are going to focus on getting Aella back."

"How? I mean, not to be Downer Debbie over here, but the Devil took her *to Hell*."

Janara shrugged. "One of us will just have to go in after her."

"And by 'one of us,' you mean—"

"Me, of course," Janara finished.

"Janara—" I began to protest. She raised a hand to cut me off.

"Kat, she's my sister. You'd do the same in my position." She gave me a knowing look, and I was immediately silenced. I hadn't told her about Del, yet the imploring glimmer in her eyes suggested that she knew. Somehow, she knew. She was a Kongelig—of course, she did.

"You and Matteo will be our first line of defense," she continued. "I don't mean to volunteer the two of you for front-line duty, but you have the strongest powers. You stand the best chance at holding off the Onemdi and the Devil while I fetch Aella, and Elena does whatever she needs to do to annul the contract. Arun will help you. As for Nina and Leo, their primary goal should be to protect Elena at all costs—yes, we need her alive in order for this plan to work; but this also isn't her fight. She shouldn't have to die because of something one of her ancestors did."

The plan was ludicrous. It wasn't possible for seven people—three Voktere, two Kongelig, one Daski, and one normal human—to fight the Devil and his army from Hell, let alone defeat them. It just wasn't possible.

Yet it was the best plan we had, which spoke volumes to the absurdity of the entire situation in which we found ourselves.

"Va bene," Matteo said softly. I glanced over at him. He wore a series of emotions on his face that mirrored my own inner turmoil—fear, determination, a hint of hope shadowed by the resignation of our impending deaths. I squeezed his arm lightly.

"Very well," Janara said, nodding once in confirmation. "We'll wait until Nina and Leo get here before summoning the Devil. I'm going to go find Arun so that we're ready when they arrive."

With that, she took off into the night, even her glistening arrows and pale hair blending into the all-encompassing darkness.

"Now, we wait," Matteo stated heavily in the ensuing silence.

We stood there for a few minutes, until the blackness of the night became almost suffocating. It didn't help that there still seemed to be eyes upon us—invisible eyes watching us, waiting. Matteo and Elena apparently felt equally unsettled, because they, like me, were incessantly shifting and fidgeting, eyes darting around nervously. After a few minutes of this, our discomfort became too great, and we sought the relative safety of one of the more brightly lit alleys. Elena settled herself on an upturned wooden crate while Matteo and I stood watch at the mouth of the narrow lane.

"Are you alright?"

I turned to look at Matteo, a bit taken aback by the sudden question despite its gentle intonations.

"I'm fine," I replied easily, focusing my attention back on the pitch-black street. But a warm hand wrapping around my own colder one sent me searching for his familiar brown eyes that were illuminated ethereally by the rich yellow lamplight.

"We'll get through this together," he assured, offering me the reassurance I didn't know I needed. Familiar tendrils of comfort flowed through me as his fingers tangled with mine. I smiled softly at the feeling, closing my eyes for a moment as I relished in the way his hand grounded me, the way his soul soothed me. Apparently, he had expertly learned the art of transferring emotions across our soulbond to calm me.

"When all this is all over, you'll have to show me how you do that."

"Do what?" he asked innocently.

"Use our bond to comfort me."

"You noticed?"

I nodded, rubbing my arms against the chill of the night air. "You should teach me so I can return the gesture."

He smiled, answering, "It will be my pleasure."

Feeling a bit more settled, I relaxed back against the stone wall behind me. With our hands still entwined—and Matteo's thumb running comforting circles along my knuckles—we turned our gazes back out into the open night air as we waited for our two-person cavalry to arrive.

And arrive they did, just as the first of twelve chimes sounded across Torcello. Janara and Arun met them at the docking point and brought them to our location.

"Ok, how do we do this?" Nina asked. She had already brought the twins up to speed on the nullification of the contract, and Janara had filled Nina and Leo in on the plan for the coming fight.

"One of us is going to need to summon the Devil," Arun said.

"And we know what happened to the last person who tried that," Leo muttered darkly.

"It can't be Janara or Arun," Nina pointed out. "They'll be trying to get through to their sister—they can't have any attention drawn to them until they make their move. Otherwise, they'll never have a chance of getting to that portal."

"I can do it," Elena volunteered. Even before she had finished speaking though, Janara was shaking her head.

"We appreciate that, but you'll be the most help to us by getting that contract amended and signed. Since that can only happen while the Devil is on Torcello, we're going to need you to get started on it as soon as he appears."

"I'll do it," I offered.

"Kat, no, you can't," Matteo immediately protested.

"It's the only option," I insisted. "Elena, Janara, and Arun *can't* be the ones to summon the Devil because it could jeopardize the other tasks they need to accomplish. Leo and Nina have to protect Elena at all costs—and it is going to take *both* of them to do that. Which leaves you and me," I stated, turning to face Matteo. "And between the two of us, you're the one with the best chance of holding off the Onemdi. You're a Salamander. You can manipulate fire, just like they can. That gives you the best shot of the two of us in holding them off. So, if one of us has to sacrifice themselves to summon the Devil... it should be me."

Logically, my reasoning was infallible. But it wasn't the only reason I was offering to be the sacrificial lamb. There was something else, something I didn't dare voice—the fact that I preferred the thought of my own demise over that of my soulmate. Of course, I didn't *want* to die, but I had realized almost as soon as I met Matteo that I would do anything to keep him safe. I just didn't think Matteo would be overly thrilled if I told him that.

Matteo opened his mouth to protest, but Janara didn't give him the chance.

"Kat's right—she has to be the one to summon the Devil." She stared long and hard at me. "Arun, do you have the candle?"

"Right here," her brother answered, sliding an oblong candle and a small holder from his inner coat pocket. He passed both objects to me. As I slid the candle into the metal holder, Janara watched me with an indecipherable expression on her face.

"Kat, don't be a martyr. Get up on that bridge, run through the summoning process, and then get out of there before that portal fully opens. We don't want the Devil getting a chance to run you through like a shish kabob the way he did with the shopkeeper's son."

I nodded mutely. It was sheer insanity—facing the Devil with nothing but a candle. Speed was the only hope

I had to survive this.

"We'll all be in position, ready to make our move. Nina, Leo, take Elena somewhere far enough away to keep her safe from the Devil, but close enough that you can still see everything going on around the bridge. We may need your help. Elena, as soon as you see the Devil step out of the portal, use that key. Either Nina or Leo will go with you. Get back to the night the contract was originally signed, and do what you need to do to amend it. But please, be careful, be thorough, and be quick."

Elena nodded. Then, Janara turned back to me and Matteo.

"Matteo, you stay close to Kat. If she gets off the bridge safely after summoning the Devil, you two are going to need to hold off the Onemdi long enough for me to get through the portal, find Aella, and get out. Arun will back you up. The moment I'm back with Aella, Elena will need to sign the revised contract. The Devil's not going to be happy about it, so be careful—I'm not sure how he'll react. But at least he won't be able to harm anyone here after that. He'll have no choice but to leave."

"Not to sound grim, but what happens if you *don't* return with your sister?" Leo asked. Nina elbowed him in the ribs, and he gave her an offended look, confused by her attack.

"Leo's right... how are we going to know if you've been successful or not?" Arun questioned. "I love you, sis, you know I do. It would kill me to lose you and Aella. But we can't hold off the Onemdi forever."

Janara pursed her lips, looking thoughtful for a moment. Then, shrugging her shoulders, she responded, "Give me thirty minutes. If we're not back in that time, sign the contract."

"A lot can happen in thirty minutes, J," Arun murmured.

"I know," Janara nodded. "But I'm asking you to at least try to hold out that long. If you can't—if it looks like Venice might be lost—then sign it sooner. But, please, try your hardest to last for as much of that half-hour as you possibly can."

"We can do it," I stated with more confidence than I felt. Janara gave me a small, grateful smile.

"Well, then, let's all get into position," she commanded, breaking the brief silence that had fallen over us. Casting a passing glance upon each of us, she added, "I'll see you all when this is over. In bocca al lupo."

With that, she tugged on Arun's arm. He gave a reluctant wave before following his sister into the darkness.

"Well, I guess, the three of us should go find our battle stations, too," Leo commented, aiming for humor but falling short. "Mio fratello," he said, clapping Matteo on the shoulder. Then, he turned his eyes on me. Stepping forward, he wrapped me in a one-armed hug, whispering, "Mia sorella." My eyes stung at the familial endearment as I returned the embrace. A moment later, Leo stepped back, huffing out a breath full of emotion. "A presto."

"A presto," Matteo rasped. "Make sure you take care of Nina and Elena."

"I will," he promised.

"And Nina," Matteo continued, shifting his gaze to my curly-haired friend. "Keep him out of trouble."

"Don't worry," she chuckled, her voice watery. "I will." Then, with pleading eyes, she requested, "Please, take care of my sister."

"Per sempre," Matteo answered sincerely, reaching for my hand and giving it a squeeze.

"Be safe," I said in a tremoring voice, my eyes falling on Elena, then Leo, and finally coming to rest on Nina. "In bocca al lupo."

"In bocca al lupo," she echoed softly. With one last meaningful look, she allowed herself to be led away by Leo, trailing alongside him and Elena as they slipped off into the night.

It felt like déjà vu—being alone with Matteo, surrounded by the crisp night air and the distant rhythmic swishing of the canals on this sleepy island. My first date with Matteo had been nearly identical—if you didn't count the whole *I might die in a few minutes at the hands of the Devil's army* thing. I looked up at the night sky, stretching out above us like a dark blanket. Millions of twinkling stars blinked back at me. It was amazing how those celestial objects always seemed to reflect what was transpiring beneath them. On my first date with Matteo, they glittered happily as they kept watch over us. But now, they flickered dimly, almost melancholically—as though they already knew of the events that were about to transpire, the sacrifices that were about to be made. And, perhaps, they did.

"Are you alright?"

My eyes fell to Matteo's face. Even in the darkness, I could see his large doe eyes observing me with such blatant worry and fear that it sent a pang through my heart. He was holding my hand firmly, as though he could keep me safe and tethered close to him—as though he could prevent the inevitability of losing me—through that single, strong grasp.

Staring into his eyes, knowing I was only minutes away from potentially being ripped from him forever... I couldn't lie. I couldn't pretend. I couldn't even try to be optimistic. Instead, I tightened my own fingers around his hand, trying to memorize the warmth and security of it. Around my wrist, our soulmark seemed to glow in the darkness.

"I don't want to lose you," I whispered thickly.

"Nor I, you," he answered passionately.

"And I don't want to leave you."

"Me either."

"But I have to do this," I continued, holding up the candle.

"Yes."

"I can't be selfish—as much as I want to be."

"No. Neither of us can be." It sounded like Matteo was about to cry, and his grip on my hand grew impossibly tighter. It wasn't painful, though. It never was.

"There's no other choice." This time, I wasn't talking about the ritual, but rather about my own self-sacrifice. And Matteo knew it.

"Yes, there is."

I looked up sharply at him.

"You come back to me." He raised his free hand to my cheek, stroking it gently. "You summon the Devil, you get off that bridge quickly, and you come back to me."

A tear slipped from my eye, and he swiped it away tenderly with his thumb.

"You're it for me, Kat. Even if we hadn't been tied together with this soulbond, you would still be the only one my heart would ever choose. You're like a cool wind on a blistering summer day, a drink of water for a man dying of dehydration, a breath of fresh air for someone trapped in the smoky depths of a blazing fire. You are my other half—you make me better, you bring out the best in me, you make me see the world in a way I had never thought to before. And I *refuse* to lose you. You are the single most important thing in my life, and I will fight to my last breath to keep you.

"I love you, Kat. Maybe it's too soon to say that since we've only known each other for a few weeks. But, we're soulmates. And right now, we're facing a life-threatening situation. So, I don't really care about formalities. I love you, and I need you to know that."

"I love you, too," I replied tearfully, pushing my cheek further into the hand cradling it. "And I'll come back to you—whatever it takes, I'll make sure we both come out of this alive."

"You'd better. After all, I still owe you an uninter-rupted first date."

I chuckled, swiping a hand across my eyes. "Yes, you do."

His lips tugged into his familiar crooked smile. "Then, when this is all over, you and I are going on a *proper* date— I promise."

"I'm going to hold you to that."

With a few last strokes of his thumb across my cheek, Matteo leaned forward and tenderly pressed his lips to mine. The kiss was bittersweet, filled with longing and sadness. When Matteo pulled away a few moments later, it was only to place an equally soft kiss on my forehead. I closed my eyes, soaking up all of the love, compassion, and respect that were poured into that single gesture.

We stayed like that for several long seconds before

Matteo sighed, reluctantly stepping back.

"Well, shall we go 'give them Hell,' as they say?"

With a breathy laugh, I swiped at my eyes, nodding. "Definitely. Let's go."

Grabbing his hand, I tugged him out of the alley. Together, we set off in the direction of Il Ponte del Diavolo.

CHAPTER SEVENTEEN

Who knew a pile of bricks could be so intimidating? To be fair, the Devil's Bridge was more of an *arch* than an actual pile, but still... it was terrifying. Standing firm over the swirling black waters the canal and backed by the silhouette of the towering campanile that stood as a quiet sentinel over Torcello, its steep stairs and almost impossibly curved crest were menacing. Knowing that the creature that served as the bridge's namesake was going to be making an appearance within the next few minutes? Well, that made it all the more daunting.

"Remember, cross the bridge twice with the candle. As soon as the portal starts to appear, get off. I don't care if you have to dive into the canal to do it. Just *get off that bridge*," Matteo reminded me sternly. I nodded in comprehension, taking a deep breath to steady my quaking nerves. He placed a hand on my arm, giving it a light squeeze. "I'm right here, Kat. I'll be here the entire time. You can do this. I know you can."

"Sì, certo," I replied, patting the hand resting on my arm. "Grazie."

We stood together in the still night air for a few moments more, before Matteo exhaled sharply. "Alright, let's light the candle."

He lifted his hand from my arm, then raised a single finger in front of him. A second later, a small flame popped up above it. I held the candle out toward him, and he brought his finger to the wick, igniting the candle.

"I'll be right over there," Matteo said, pointing toward a corner where two stone buildings met, the area shrouded in heavy shadows and cluttered with barrels and stacks of wooden crates.

"Ok," I murmured.

"I'll be waiting for you," he promised. Then, with a nod of encouragement, he retreated into his hiding place. I waited until he was safely concealed before turning to face the bridge.

I glanced down at the candle in my hands. It was almost hypnotizing to watch the tiny flame flickering back and forth, little beads of wax rolling down the shaft of the candle to escape the heat. The dancing flame was Matteo's own creation, and in a way, it was comforting to know that I was carrying a part of him with me.

Taking a deep breath, I placed one foot on the first step of the bridge. Then another. Step by step, I ascended the stairs to the top of the structure, moving fluidly across the crest of it to the other side. My heart hammered loudly in my ears, the candle in my hands trembling slightly as my hands shook. Descending the stairs on the opposite side of the bridge, I started my return journey.

I had just barely made it to the top of the bridge for the second time before an orange spark leapt up in front of me. Then, a few more fluttered through the air. I quickened my pace, scurrying down the flight of precipitous stairs just as I heard the familiar roar of the portal opening behind me.

As soon as my feet hit the brick path again, I sprinted toward Matteo, who was still obscured by the crates and shadows. He eagerly reached out for me as soon as I was close enough and pulled me down beside him. He placed a comforting hand on my back, and I placed one of my own over my chest in an attempt to slow my racing heart. Shifting closer to him, I peered out at the bridge through one of the gaps between the crates.

In the middle of the bridge, churning angrily in a vicious circle of orange and yellow, was the portal. It swirled ominously, like a whirlpool of flames threatening to consume anyone who dared to venture too close.

A few moments later, a figure emerged from that blazing doorway between our realm and Hell. By now, the creature was frighteningly familiar—with his gray skin, black horns, red eyes, flowing robes, and blazing pitchfork.

"Who summoned me?" the Devil asked, glancing around the vacant area surrounding the bridge. When there was no response, he raised his voice. "*Who summoned me?*" he thundered loudly, his irritated voice echoing across the empty island.

There r
a gentle nudge against my side from Matteo. He nodded toward the bridge, indicating that it was time to move. Even in the inky thickness of the night,

I could see him mouth the words, "Don't get too close." Nodding, I stood from my hiding place, snuck around the crates and barrels, and emerged from the shadows.

Walking across those brick paving stones felt like stepping into no man's land. And, in a way, I supposed I was—the enemy in front of me, the safety of cover and support behind me, and nothing but open space and the fragile peace of ceasefire around me. My mind screamed at me to go back, my heart pounding its own support of the idea. Still, I continued on, each footfall carrying me closer to the Devil looming large on the bridge before me.

The Devil watched my approach with intense scrutiny. I didn't dare look at him, but I could feel those red eyes boring into me. Goosebumps tingled across my skin. When I had neared the foot of the bridge but was still far enough from the Devil to not be skewered by his pitchfork, I stopped. Summoning every ounce of courage still within me, I raised my head defiantly and met his intrigued gaze with a hard stare of my own.

"I did," I stated boldly, forcing myself to remain unflinching in the face of the Devil's sinister presence. He narrowed his eyes, observing me closely. It was like he was searching for something, reading the lines of a book that only he could see. The seconds ticked by. I could feel myself start to sweat, growing increasingly nervous—but I didn't dare move. I barely even breathed. Then, after what felt like an eternity, those red orbs widened infinitesimally, the ashen face morphing into something akin to curiosity.

"Ah, I see. And what it is that has led you to summon me? I can see that you are not here to provide Venice's much-delayed payment for my *services* two centuries ago. Though, at least you seem to possess more intelligence than that fool who tried to trick me with the goats."

I flinched at the memory, trying not to think about the fact that I was currently standing in the exact spot that the body of the shopkeeper's son had fallen only a couple of weeks ago. Was it just my imagination, or were the bricks beneath my feet still stained with the red tint of his blood? I felt nauseous.

"Hmm..." the Devil hummed, rubbing his black goatee as he considered me. "No tricks, but no genuine payment either." He dropped his hand, tilting his head as a sadistic smile spread across his face, his razor-sharp teeth glinting in the flickering light of the portal behind him. "So, why is it that a Daski, of all people, has seen fit to summon me back to Venice?"

I swallowed thickly, suddenly feeling like an ice-cold hand had clenched my insides in a vice-like grip. How did the Devil know that I was a Daski? What did that mean for us? For our plan?

Knowing there wasn't time to dwell on the potential "what-ifs" now, I pushed ahead with our original scheme, casting a silent prayer to the Norns that this would somehow work.

"I brought you here to tell you to leave Venezia," I answered, surprised by how firm I managed to keep my voice. "You have no claim over this city or its people. The contract you made with Maria Pesaro doesn't matter. She was *one* woman, and that was over two hundred years ago. You have no right to punish the entire city, or the people who live here, for Maria's failure to uphold her end of the contract. These people, these modern Venetians... they've done nothing to you. They're innocent."

"Are they now?" he asked sardonically. "Perhaps they

did not each sign the contract as Signorina Pesaro did, but it was the narrow-mindedness of their ancestors that led her to summon me to her aid in the first place. You see, she just wanted to be with her one true love. But did they allow her to do so? No—and all because he was Austrian. He was *the enemy*. I would hardly call prejudice like that *innocence*.

"Ah, but I can see by your face that you think me wrong. Do you disagree that they were wrong to keep dear Maria away from her beloved Franz? She was a woman with the rare perception to overlook political loyalties and see the person lying beneath them."

I said nothing, simply glaring up at the Devil as he grinned maliciously.

"No—you don't disagree, do you? Instead, you take issue with the fact that I want to punish *these* particular Venetians," he continued, gesturing around Torcello with his hands. "But I wonder—why are you so determined to protect these so-called *innocent* people, when you know they haven't changed? Do you not recognize the bigotry and judgment that lingers in their hearts? Do you not realize that it is humanity's greatest weakness that they criticize and condemn and *hate* others who are different— who see the world differently, who live differently, who look or behave differently from themselves?"

He paused, lowering his voice as he peered down at me.

"Do you not think that they wouldn't hesitate to turn their backs on *you*, if they knew what you truly are? Do you think they would still want you here, these *innocent* people? Do you think they would live contentedly alongside you, welcome you, befriend you if they knew all that you are, all that you are capable of doing?"

I gulped, eyes widening and breathing becoming ragged as the Devil easily found the weak spots lingering in my heart, striking them blow after blow.

"I think you know the truth: that Venetians today—that *people* today—are no different than they were back then. I think you know that they'd never want you or accept your presence in their *precious* city if they knew what you are. And I can't help but wonder..." he again scratched his goatee. "Why would a Daski—a *monster*—like you want to defend a group of people that wouldn't hesitate to slaughter you in the most painful way they know how, as though they were righteous slayers driving a wooden stake through the heart of a vampire?"

I froze. My mouth opened and closed, but I couldn't think of a thing to say. It was like my mind had suddenly become a broken record, playing the Devil's words over and over on repeat in my head.

A Daski.... A monster... Wouldn't hesitate to slaughter you...

"Because she's *not* a monster," came a strong, and surprisingly furious voice beside me. "She's a good person who knows the difference between right and wrong. She'll protect this city and the people in it, flaws and all, regardless of the cost—just as I will—because it is the right thing to do. You call her a monster, but as far as I'm concerned, the only monster around here is *you*."

I gaped at Matteo, who had wrapped a strong hand around my own. If the stakes of the situation hadn't been so dire, I might have laughed. Only Matteo—dear, sweet, kind, gentle, sympathetic, understanding, couldn't-say-a-bad-word-about-another-living-creature   Matteo—would tell the Devil straight to his face that he was a monster.

Even the Devil seemed shocked by this turn of events. He blinked at Matteo, momentarily struck silent. His red eyes flickered down to our joined hands, then jumped to my face before shifting back to Matteo.

"A Salamander and a Daski? Soulmates? How is that possible?" he asked in a voice that was filled with something akin to awe.

"What? Are you surprised that there are forces in the world more powerful than you?" Matteo sniped, and I gave his hand a soft tug, silently pleading with him to not press his luck.

"Who are you two?" the Devil snapped, scowling at us.

"We're the defenders of this city—the two Vaettir who have been entrusted by fate to ensure that you don't hurt a single person here," Matteo responded firmly. I had no idea how he was so calm and confident about everything. I was all but quaking in my boots.

"Are you now?" the Devil questioned mockingly. "And just what do you think you're going to do to stop me? You are but two pathetic Vaettir. *I* am Lucifer, Prince of the Underworld—and I have the powers of Hell on my side."

With those words, the Devil spread his arms wide, and the portal once more flared to life. In their organized rows, the Onemdi emerged. They floated down the stairs, their thick cloaks fluttering with their movements. Matteo and I shifted closer to each other, our hands tightening their hold on each other as the demons surrounded us in a wide circle.

"I seem to remember you two now," the Devil said, descending the stairs of the bridge as he eyed us with amusement. "You were here the last time I appeared in

Venice—when I was summoned by those two fools with the goats." He approached nearer, walking slow laps around us like a predator stalking its prey.

"We were there the time before that, too," Matteo spoke up hotly. "We seem to be around every time you terrorize, threaten, or kill innocent people here on Torcello."

The Devil stopped in front of Matteo, an evil smirk stretching wide across his face.

"You have a boldness of spirit... perhaps recklessly so." My heart clenched in fear as the Devil's features took on a dangerous look—well, more dangerous. "But you have powers that make up for your foolishly misguided loyalties. I saw the way you fought during my last visit here—it was quite impressive." He slowly closed the distance between himself and Matteo. The Adam's apple in Matteo's throat bobbed nervously, and a trill of terror rippled through the bond—but beyond that, there was no expression of nervousness on Matteo's part. He remained resolute, even when there was less than a foot of cold night air between him and the hellish prince.

"I could use someone like you on our side," the Devil continued. "I could offer you power and riches beyond your wildest imagination. All you need to do is offer your soul and your loyalty to *me*."

The muscles in Matteo's jaw clenched.

"No?" the Devil asked with feigned disappointment. "Well, that's too bad. Perhaps your friend here would be more willing."

The Devil then turned his full attention upon me. There was a sharp intake of breath from beside me. And suddenly, where momentary fear had flitted through our soulbond only seconds ago, now there was complete panic. "After all, she's the one with the heart of ice."

The Devil moved in front of me, eyeing me closely like one would an interesting artifact in a museum exhibit.

"A Daski—rare and valuable, like a diamond." He cocked his head, his eyes gleaming. "If you were to join forces with me, you could become great. I could give you the power to do incredible things—power that you've always been denied by society, by your family. You would be unstoppable..."

"Keep dreaming," I hissed. The Devil smirked.

"Ah, you're rather feisty—a true characteristic of a Daski." He took a step back, shaking his head. "It's a shame. I could make you so much more than you are now. You have so much potential. Alas," he sighed. "Now, you'll die—just like the rest of them. And your powers—your glorious powers—will be wasted. What a pity."

Turning on his heel, he stalked back toward the bridge.

"Kat, now!" Matteo whispered just loud enough for me to hear. Extending my hand, ice shot out from my fingertips, coating the ground around us with ice. I forced the tendrils of ice forward, creeping rapidly along the bricks until they reached the bridge and began to climb the stairs step by step. Finally, the ice caught up to the Devil. Unaware of what was transpiring behind—and now beneath—him, the Devil placed his foot on the last step before reaching the top of the bridge. Without traction on the steep stairs, his foot slipped, sending him spiraling ungracefully into the waters of the canal below.

As soon as we heard the *splash*, several things happened at once.

A ring of fire sprang up from the ground behind the

Onemdi, trapping us in the circle of fire with them.

Outraged that their commander had been targeted, the Onemdi materialized their whips of fire. They lashed out at me and Matteo from all directions, the two of us ducking and dodging the crackling flames.

There was a bright flash of light. Then, off to my left, a shadow—tall and slim—rushed through the darkness behind the perimeter of flames. It reached the bridge, flying up the melting steps. With only a brief glimpse of its white-blonde hair, the figure disappeared into the portal.

And somewhere behind us, a voice filled with a mixture of frustration and horror yelled out, "Arun!"

I couldn't give any of these things too much thought, however, for Matteo and I were now engaged in a fight to the death with the Devil's army. Tongues of flames whizzed past us, scorching through the chilly December air. Matteo flung balls of fire from his hands, hitting a few Onemdi who screeched inhumanly in anger. I reached out, coating the ground once more in ice, sending a few Onemdi sliding across the brick pathway. But the fiery perimeter was growing too high, its heat melting the ice almost instantaneously.

Realizing that such a defensive tactic was no longer going to be useful, there were very few options remaining as I watched the Onemdi regaining their footing and rushing towards us once more. So, conjuring icy daggers in my hands, I spun around, flinging them at the Onemdi. The jagged knives pierced their targets. The Onemdi that were struck by them froze. An angry hissing emanated from their bodies as the daggers chilled their fiery cores, and I tried desperately to swallow the bile that rose to my throat at the sound. Then, their bodies evaporated in bursts of steam and flurries of ash.

As Matteo and I were battling the Onemdi, I spotted movement out of the corner of my eye. I turned just in time to see a dark figure leap over the ring of fire, bow and arrow poised at the ready, and blonde braid glistening with an orange hue in the flickering light from the flames. The crack of a whip in my ear startled me, and without thinking, I swirled around and threw another dagger toward the demon that was advancing on me, the icy blade penetrating its chest just as Janara's arrow impaled the cloaked torso an inch to the right.

"Janara, what are you doing here?" I shouted, throwing a spiked ball of ice at an Onemdi trying to sneak up on Matteo from behind. "I thought you were going through the portal to find Aella!"

"Arun blinded me with a solar flare," she yelled back, shooting off another arrow. "He went into the portal instead." There was another streak of a pale blue arrow flying past me, and then Janara's furious voice roaring, "If he survives this, I'm going to kill the idiot!"

Despite the fact that we were in the middle of a battle, I couldn't help the smirk that tugged at my lips. I hurled another dagger of ice at an Onemdi lurking near the fiery perimeter.

No sooner had the icy blade left my hand than a searing heat crashed into my side. I spiraled through the air, landing roughly on my back on the solid ground. A muffled groan escaped my lips as my mind tried to catch up with the stinging pain in my side and the unplanned flight I had just taken across the brick pathway.

"Kat!" In that single syllable, there was more terror than I ever wanted to hear in my soulmate's voice. It was accompanied by an overwhelming, gut-wrenching torrent of worry, fear, and blinding rage flooding through our soulbond.

The night sky above me was interspersed with streaks of orange flames and blue ice. The air was filled with the horrible shrieking and hissing of the Onemdi as they were hit by Matteo's fire and Janara's arrows. I laid there, dazed, watching the colors as they flashed across the stars and listening to the distant sounds of battle around me. The next thing I knew, Matteo was by my side, his face entering my field of vision. He knelt over me, his warm hands cupping my face.

"Kat," he breathed.

"I'm okay," I croaked, sitting up with a wince.

"Where are you hurt?" he questioned frantically, his eyes scanning me for signs of injury.

"Just my side," I answered, one hand subconsciously moving to cover the burn on my torso.

"Let me see," he murmured, his own hands reaching to check the injured area. However, at that moment, I happened to look up—and what I saw made my heart clench in fear.

Behind Matteo was an Onemdi, looming large, its claw-like hand outstretched toward us as fire leapt from its hand. Matteo must have seen the alarm on my face, because he immediately started to turn, raising his hands. But with the close proximity of the Onemdi and the speed at which the stream of fire was traveling, I knew he wouldn't be able to turn quickly enough to defend himself.

There was a fleeting moment where I recognized what I had to do. It was something that had once cost me a sister, a family, my own self-respect...

It was something that had once proven that I was the monster the world had always expected me to be.

But now, it was my only way of protecting the single most important person in my life. And when it came to protecting Matteo, I would go to the ends of the Earth. I'd move Heaven and Hell. I'd break a million promises to myself time and again, and spend an eternity hating myself for it.

Just so long as it kept him safe.

So, just as Matteo started to spin toward the Onemdi, I pushed myself off of the ground, shoving him to the side, my hands already raising instinctively. Digging down deep, I searched for the core of my energy and pushed it through my hands as quickly as I could. I felt the ice racing through my veins and leaping from my body to materialize in front of me. It continued to build and grow—crystallizing, expanding, solidifying—until a thick wall of ice stood between us and the demon. Time seemed to be passing in slow motion as I watched the ice shield form, but in reality, neither Matteo nor I had hardly taken a breath.

The fire slammed into the shield, and I shuddered slightly at the force of the impact. Bracing my feet on the ground and gritting my teeth, I shoved even more of my energy into the shield. Ice continued to pile up, thickening the shield layer by layer. The light from the flames flickered dully on the other side, the energy from the heat radiating through the ice and into my very being. Water pooled on the bricks as the fire melted the shield at its point of impact. It was painful and exhausting, but still, I held firm, pouring as much ice and energy into the shield as I possibly could.

I had to protect Matteo.

Suddenly, there was a large explosion, a massive wave of fire smashing into the shield, ricocheting off, and rippling across the area. The repercussion crashed into the Onemdi, all of their cloaks simultaneously igniting in their own hellish fires. A series of unified, ear-piercing shrieks reverberated through the night as the demons were consumed by the flames. Within seconds, the skeletal figures and their black robes were reduced to clouds of gray ash that were carried away by the wind.

"No!" came the enraged cry of the Devil, who, at some point, had clambered out of the canal. A bolt of red light flew from his pitchfork, slamming into my shield and shattering it. I sagged, falling into Matteo who instinctively covered my body with his as shards of ice rained down upon us. The ice tinkled as it smashed against the bricks, breaking into countless minuscule pieces like glass.

Looking up, we saw the Devil advancing toward us. Janara had rushed to our side as soon as my shield shattered, and now had her bow raised, arrow poised and aimed directly at the Devil. Matteo pulled me closer to him, recognizing my limpness as a sign of magical exhaustion. He knew I was too tired to continue fighting.

The Devil raised his pitchfork again, and—

"Stop!"

I nearly sobbed in relief at the sound of Leo's voice. We all turned, seeing Nina, Leo, and Elena sprinting in our direction.

"Now what?" the Devil snapped.

"You can't harm them!" Nina cried.

"Why not?" questioned the Devil with a bitter chuckle.

"Because you have no claim over this city or its people

any longer," Elena replied firmly.

"You are mistaken. You see, I have a contract—"

"*Had* a contract," Leo corrected snidely. A flicker of worry passed across the Devil's red eyes.

"The contract you signed is broken," Nina added.

"Broken?" the Devil hissed. "Impossible!"

"Actually, it's not," Nina replied with a certain sass that she had definitely picked up from Leo. Even in my exhaustion, I smiled at her boldness. "Your contracts are signed in blood, and can only be altered or signed by the person whose blood was used to sign it... or someone who shares their blood."

"We found one of Maria Pesaro's descendants," she continued, gesturing toward Elena. "She went back using the Key of Time, added a nullifying clause to the contract, and signed it."

Elena waved the key in the air with a bandaged hand, just as Nina held up the signed contract for the Devil to see. Sure enough, at the bottom of the nearly-crumbling paper was a series of lines in a scrawl that didn't match the rest of the document. Beside it, in bright red blood that still glistened with wetness, was Elena's neat signature.

"I didn't sign that!" the Devil roared. I frowned, turning my gaze back to the fuming creature.

"Actually, you did," Leo retorted lazily. "Right after I distracted you so that Elena could add the addendum before you signed it."

The Devil blinked. He blinked again. And then, his face twisted into something ugly and malevolent. "Trickery!" he bellowed loudly.

He raised his pitchfork, flames spouting from the tips of it. Leo's eyes widened, before he hastily pushed Nina and Elena behind him, shielding them. Janara pulled the string on her bow taught, taking aim at the Devil once more. I clung desperately to Matteo, who wrapped his arm tighter around me, raising his free hand as a few sparks flew from his fingers. The Devil growled, the flames growing brighter—

And then he was gone—flung across the brick pathway by a terrific gust of wind. He slammed hard into the stone wall of a building and crashed into the pile of crates behind which Matteo and I had sought cover earlier that evening. We all stared in confusion at the broken wood from the crates and the inelegant pile of robes that was the Devil. With mirrored looks of complete bewilderment, we turned in the direction from which the wind had come.

Standing at the top of the bridge was Arun. And perched on his hip, with white-blonde hair in a braid identical to her sister's, was Aella.

"He's really annoying," came her musical voice in explanation, accompanied by an indifferent shrug.

"Wouldn't you know that our sister is a Sylph?" Arun exclaimed cheerily, setting the small girl on her feet. Aella hurried down the wet stairs with bewildering grace, rushing toward Janara and flinging her arms around her elder sister's waist. Janara let out a huff—and if there was a glimmer of tears in her eyes, I pretended I didn't see it— then scooped her sister up, hugging her close. Arun casually strolled over to us, pulling out his own bow.

"Well, it looks like all the excitement is over, huh?" he asked, looking around at the empty streets and dying flames. Then, his eyes flickered to me and Matteo, shifted to Nina, Elena, and Leo who were still huddled closely together, and finally landed back on his two sisters. "And we all made it out in one piece!"

For some reason, *that* seemed to be what made Janara snap. She looked up sharply, putting Aella down and instructing her to stand near me and Matteo. Then, she took several deliberate steps toward her brother, closing the gap between them.

"J, you should've seen it, I—"

Whatever Arun had been about to say was cut short by the collision of Janara's fist with his mouth. He stumbled back a few steps, his eyes wide as he gazed at his sister in shock. He brought one hand up, wiping away the small trace of blood that had appeared there.

"What the *bloody hell* was that for?" he squawked.

"You know damn well what that was for," she retorted harshly. "Don't play innocent with me. You purposefully blinded me with a solar flare so that *you* would be the one to go through that portal instead of me!"

"I don't get why you're so upset! I have sunlight to fight with. In case you've forgotten, the Onemdi *hate* sunlight—it burns them just as well as fire and destroys them with the same efficiency as ice."

"That's not the point! I was trying to protect you, you bloody idiot!" she shouted, shoving him in the shoulder.

"And *I* was trying to protect *you!*"

Janara looked like she had been slapped in the face, and all of the fight seemed to drain out of her in an instant. Shaking her head with a quiet huff of disbelief, she stepped forward and wrapped her brother in a tight embrace. Arun seemed momentarily shocked by his sister's rare show of physical affection, but quickly relaxed and returned her hug.

Seeing the two twins together, with Nina, Leo, and

Elena on one side of them and Aella, Matteo, and myself on the other... the reality that we had actually won began to sink in. It was overwhelming. Going into this night, we had nothing but a risky plan and a hope for the least number of casualties possible. Yet, by some miracle, not only had we all survived, but we had also achieved *both* of our goals—we got Aella back safely, and we broke the Devil's contract.

I wanted to jump for joy. Or cry. Or maybe both. We had *actually* done it. It was finally over.

A frustrated grumbling and the banging of wooden shards drew our attention back to the dark corner. The Devil, who had been temporarily stunned by Aella's attack, had finally recovered and was now clambering out of the pile of debris. He stumbled from the hodge-podge of wood, metal, and... was that *jam*?

Aella snickered at the gooey purple substance coating part of the Devil's robes. Yup, she had sent him crashing into a crate full of grape jelly. I bit my lower lip, trying not to laugh. There was no need to instigate him even further.

"How dare you," the Devil hissed. Janara and Arun rushed forward, standing in front of us with their bows raised, ready for another attack. Leo raised his hands, a few large chunks of earth floating over from somewhere on the other side of the canal. Nina spread her hands wide, the waters in the canal swishing violently and then rising in a threatening wall.

"How dare you!" the Devil roared, staggering forward a few steps and raising his pitchfork once more. Leo's boulders of earth started to spin in preparation for their assault. Nina's wall of water curved forward, ready to crash down on its intended target. Matteo held out one hand, a ball of fire swirling in his palm. Janara and Arun pulled back the strings of their bows, their movements identical, and their respective blue and yellow arrows primed for flight. Around us, a light breeze was progressively picking up speed, gusting wildly through the tight alleys of Torcello.

That was when, with a loud rumble, the portal flared to life once more, burning brighter than a thousand suns.

And another figure stepped out.

CHAPTER EIGHTEEN

It took a moment for the blinding flare from the portal to die down—but as soon as it did, we all turned our eyes to it. A woman stood in front of the spinning flames, having just emerged from the inter-realm gateway. She was tall and slender, but the way she held herself radiated elegance and power. With sharp features that spoke to an underlying intelligence, and piercing black eyes that examined the world with an authoritative aloofness, her entire being was the epitome of regality.

Unlike the Devil, the woman before us had ghostly pale skin that was harshly juxtaposed by her long, dark hair. Cascading over her shoulders like an obsidian waterfall, the straight black strands were offset by a single streak of red that matched her crimson lips. As though to complete the look, even her dress consisted of ombre shades of black and red.

Yet despite her natural beauty, there was something disconcerting about her appearance...

For starters, the fact that she looked like a decomposing corpse.

At first glance, she appeared human—like a person you might meet on the street. But on closer inspection, the skin on her arms and hands was mottled, as though acid had eaten away parts of the flesh. Beneath, pearly white bones were revealed. It reminded me of the skeletal Onemdi.

A shiver ran through me, but I couldn't bring myself to look away from her equally attractive and disturbing figure. As her onyx eyes scanned the scene with an odd combination of interest and detachment, another cloaked figure stepped out of the portal to stand beside her. I immediately tensed, expecting it to be another fire demon. But I relaxed slightly—and only slightly—when I noticed that the figure's silver staff was clutched by human-like hands, not bony claws.

"Well, well, what have we here?" the woman asked, like a mother confronting a child who had just done something wrong.

"My queen," the Devil said in acknowledgment. My eyes widened as he bowed low to her. "The mortals of Venice broke a contract with me. I have merely come to collect my debt."

"Really?" Keeping her gaze affixed on him, she descended the stairs and approached him with a grace that was both beautiful and intimidating. The Devil straightened, tension evident in his stature. "It was my understanding that the contract had just been revoked."

"A trick, my queen," the Devil insisted, his ruby eyes flashing.

"Come now, Lucifer," she said with a disapproving look in her eyes. "I am the queen of the Underworld—do you not think I see all and know all that transpires in relation to it?"

The Devil cringed minutely at the reminder and, as she continued to scrutinize him, seemed to shrink.

"My queen, you don't understand. These Vaettir—"

"Enough!" she bellowed, raising one of her half-flesh, half-bone hands to silence him. "You have wasted enough of my time with your foolish antics—your illegitimate son in New Jersey, that infernal fiddling contest in Georgia, the mounds of dirt you dropped in England, not to mention the ridiculous amount of bridges you've created across the seven continents in exchange for human souls. Surely they would circle the Earth several times if laid end to end." She circled him slowly, like a predator cornering its prey, a mischievous gleam in her eyes. "Though from what I've heard, the fiddling didn't quite work out in your favor. Tell me—how did it feel to lose the beloved golden fiddle that you *begged* me to make for you?"

The Devil snarled, opening his mouth with an angry retort. But at the glare he received from the woman, he immediately fell silent again, and his shoulders sagged in defeat.

"I am done with your games," she hissed, and the ground seemed to tremble with her words. "You will be returning to the Underworld with me and will resume the role that I assigned to you. Otherwise, I will gladly strip you of your powers and cast you out of our realm. Never forget that *I* am the one who bestowed you with all that you have now."

"But my queen, the contract—"

"The contract is null and void," she stated bluntly, her tone leaving no room for argument. "It was done properly. You were outwitted. It is as plain and simple as that." Then, in a low voice that held an unspoken threat, she added, "You have no more business with these people."

"Yes, your highness," the Devil mumbled as he bowed his head, duly chastised. The woman eyed him for a moment longer, then nodded in satisfaction.

"Now," she said, turning her attention to our small, eight-person group. "Let's have a look at these interesting Vaettir that so cleverly outsmarted you, shall we?" She stalked over to us. "I am Hela, goddess of the Underworld."

"Hela?" Nina gasped.

"Ah, so you've heard of me?" Hela replied with a pleased grin. "Though, I'd be rather concerned if you hadn't."

"Why are you here?" Nina bit out.

"Hmm, so rude. You're different than you used to be. Not as subdued anymore, are you?" At Nina's flabbergasted look, Hela's toothy smile widened. "Oh, yes, my dear—I know all about you... and your friends. An Undine, who lived her life happily inside books until our wayward prince over there—" she jabbed her thumb in the Devil's direction, "—decided it was time to collect on his debt."

"Then, you were taught to see the world in an entirely different way, by a Gnome with very little self-control." She tilted her head toward Leo, who still had the audacity, despite the situation, to splutter out an undignified huff of protest. "Oh, darling, you're a Gnome. Get over it," she stated in a condescending croon. "Though I must admit that I'm rather surprised by your spirit. Usually, Gnomes are much more... placid. Your fiery personality is better suited to someone like your elder brother."

Hela turned toward Matteo, a wicked smile pulling at her lips. "But then, I suspect those Salamander qualities show most predominantly in his temper." She advanced toward him, and something fiercely protective bubbled up inside of me. I tamped it down, for the time being, not wanting to make matters worse by overreacting. It wasn't like I could do much anyway—my side tugged painfully any time I moved, and my magic was drained.

"You are quite an intriguing Salamander, aren't you?" she asked. "You possess a great deal of power that is truly impressive in its strength. You could destroy worlds with a swipe of your hand. But your abilities are tamed by the iron control you maintain over them. That is rare for the fire Vaettir. Usually, they are much more volatile creatures." Her eyes drifted to his left hand, which tightened its defensive hold on my arm. Then, they wandered down to my own left hand wrapped loosely around my injured side. Her black eyes widened infinitesimally, sparkling.

"Could it be that a soulbond is the cause of your unique constraint? And a soulbond with a Daski, no less. You really are the black sheep of your kind, aren't you?" Hela smirked, her gaze fixating on me.

"You aren't exactly typical for your nature, either. You're different—so very different—from any other Daski I've ever met. So many have joined my forces throughout the years. They are always the perfect soldiers—brutal, with nearly unstoppable powers and cold hearts that lacked any empathy for the lives they took. What commander could ask for anything more?"

"But you, my dear, are truly special. The powers that I

can sense flowing through your veins would put even my best Daski warriors to shame. Not to mention, they make your boyfriend's powers look positively pathetic. If you were to join my armies, we would be undefeatable. I would possess even greater control over the mortal world— and you, of course, would receive anything you desired in return for your service."

"I'll never serve you," I ground out. She clucked her tongue in disapproval.

"So certain of yourself. Yet, you haven't even given yourself time to consider my offer."

"I don't need time," I snapped. "I will *never* join you or your armies."

"Are you sure about that?" Hela questioned mockingly, stretching a mottled hand toward me. I batted the limb away, trying not to think about the feel of rotting flesh and smooth bone that I felt against my palm as I touched her. I didn't have much time to consider it anyway, because no sooner had I swatted away the offending limb than the figure on the bridge lowered its silver scepter and sent a dark blue light streaking in my direction. It slammed into me, striking me in the abdomen before I could even register it. I doubled over, falling to the ground as the air rushed from my lungs with an *oomph*.

Immediately, the world around me gave way to blinding pain. I was no longer aware of Matteo, who had dropped to his knees beside me. Nor was I aware of our friends who were looking on with concern and consternation; or Hela and her indifferent expression; or the cloaked figure that had just shot me. Even the hard, cold bricks beneath my hands and knees were no longer able to be comprehended by my mind. The only thing I could focus on was the burning hot pain that rippled through my head in throbbing waves. It pushed against the inside of my skull, like the blast from an explosion that had nowhere to escape. The stabbing aches seared through my eyes, radiated through my muscles, and pierced through to the deepest marrow of my bones.

"—at!" Somewhere in the back of my consciousness, the single syllable broke through the pain. But I couldn't quite decipher why the sound was recognizable or important. What I *did* know was that everything hurt. My head pounded, my limbs were shaky and weak, my ears felt like they were stuffed with cotton that muffled the world around me, and even my teeth tingled with agonizing discomfort.

"Ka—" There it was again. Different letters that nevertheless nagged at me with a meaning I still couldn't quite grasp. But the sound was closer this time, the voice more recognizable. I clenched my jaw against the pain, waiting as the repeated eruptions of excruciating pain gradually dissipated.

"Kat!" The sharp, frantic exclamation chased away the remnants of the shroud that had been clouding my mind. I became aware of something cold, hard, and smooth beneath my palms. Bricks. Countering it was a warm pressure on my back—the soothing touch comforting in its familiarity. Focusing on the warmth, I allowed it to serve as an anchor to ground me. After what felt like ages, the final tendrils of pain finally slipped away, and the world faded back into focus.

I took several deep breaths, trying to stave off the nausea that assaulted me. As the threat of a rebelling stomach abated, I was able to focus more of my attention on my surroundings. The swishing of water in the canal, the cold of the air, the presence of other people near me. Riding out one final wave of queasiness, I raised my head. My gray eyes locked with Matteo's chocolate ones. They were brimming with sheer terror and panic. His face was contorted with lines of worry. I reached toward him, my hand trembling; and it was caught in a firm grasp a moment later by the hand that Matteo had just removed from my back.

"Are you alright?" he murmured, gripping my fingers firmly. I nodded weakly, unable to speak. My muscles spasmed uncontrollably, and a few tears leaked from the corners of my eyes. He wiped them away tenderly. Then, he shifted beside me so that he could pull me close to him—one hand still clasped securely around mine, the other running calming fingers through my hair as I shook in his arms.

"What did you do to her?" he roared. I burrowed my face into his chest.

"Oh, nothing you need to worry yourself with," came the cold, dismissive answer from the shadowy depths of the cloak. The voice stirred something in me, but I couldn't place it amidst the dull pounding in my head.

"You bully!" The enraged shout shattered the silence like a bat against a window, making me flinch. It was followed immediately by a strong gust of wind that rushed over the brick pathway and flung itself toward the bridge. A moment later, the cloaked figure was sent flying from the top of the structure. It tumbled through the air, hitting the ground with a muffled *thud* where it lay sprawled on the ground on the opposite side of the canal.

For a few seconds, the Earth seemed to hold its breath.

The figure seemed stunned by the impact, lying unmoving where it had fallen. But then, it jumped up quickly, lowering its scepter once more to point this time at the person who had just attacked it—Aella.

The imminent threat didn't seem to bother the youngest of our small band. She stood there, hands clenched into fists, staring down the cloaked figure across the canal. Her verdigris eyes bore the same ferocity as her sister's, and the tips of her braided hair fluttered in the agitated breeze thrashing around her. She was four feet of angry, fiery—or perhaps blustery was a more adequate description—blondness. Quite frankly, she was terrifying— and I wasn't even the one on the receiving end of her wrath.

As soon as the cloaked figure took aim at Aella, Janara and Arun swung their bows around in its direction. Two arrows—one of glittering light, the other of ice—stood ready to take flight toward their hooded target. Leo and Nina moved to stand beside the twins, blocking Aella, Matteo, and myself from the figure's view. Both were posed in fighting stances, ready for another battle. Matteo observed the scene with hawkish eyes, but he didn't move from my side. His grip on my hand remained steady, and his fingers never hesitated as they continued to comb through my hair.

Hela stepped between the cloaked figure and our little group, raising a hand. Everyone understood the movement for what it was—a signal for all parties involved to cease and desist. No one attempted to attack, but neither did they lower their weapons or relax their combative postures.

Ignoring them, Hela eyed Aella, smiling wickedly.

"You have quite the spirit," she purred in admiration. "Not to mention, brash fearlessness. You stand here, unflinching, ready to fight my personal guard. And from what I've heard," she smirked, "you weren't afraid of Lucifer, either. If the rumors are true, you made quite a mess of Lucifer's little corner of Hell during your imprisonment there."

"Your highness—" the Devil protested, clearly offended by the reminder. Seven pairs of eyes swiveled to look at him—only Janara kept hers affixed on Hela's guard. Judging by our mirrored looks of surprise, we had all forgotten the Devil was still on the island with us.

"Silence!" Hela roared. "If you speak once more, I will permanently gag you." The Devil fell silent. He did, however, send his queen a disdainful scowl. In return, Hela leveled a simmering glare upon him until he ducked his head in admonishment once more. Then, she turned back to Aella.

"Your boldness is a highly desirable quality. But such audacity can quickly become foolishness if you do not learn a bit of control. You had best learn that lesson soon from your siblings."

Shifting her attention to the two Kongeligs, she eyed them closely. "You two have done your ancestors proud with your fighting prowess today. Although, I suppose I would be remiss to ask if either of *you* would care to become warriors of the Underworld."

"You're bloody right, you would be," Janara replied frigidly. Hela tutted, shaking her head.

"Yet another peculiarity," she commented absently. "An Ullr with a warm heart, and a Vali that is not blinded by egotism or pride. As twins, you balance each other out.

Much like your friends' powers—" she gestured toward me and Matteo, "are balanced by their soulbond."

"What an odd group we have here," she murmured thoughtfully, scanning each of us with bottomless black eyes that seemed to stare right through our cores without ever actually seeing us. She tapped her chin with one long, bony finger. "Even I, as a goddess, had never deemed Vaettir like these possible." With a final disappointed clucking of her tongue, she lamented once more, "Such a pity."

"Not all hope is lost, though," she decided confidently, her eyes suddenly flickering to mine as I peered out from where I was cradled against Matteo's chest. The obsidian depths held my own gray gaze in their clutches, and I found myself unable to look away. "We'll meet again one day soon, I'm sure. Maybe then, you'll change your mind about joining me."

Giving me a knowing smile that left me with an unsettled feeling in my gut, she spun on her heel and made her way back to the bridge. Ascending the stairs, she paused at the mouth of the portal.

"Oh, and clean up the mess you made before returning to the Underworld." The words were tossed lazily over her shoulder at the Devil. Without waiting for a response, she stepped through the spinning flames, followed closely by her cloaked guard.

As soon as Hela and her guard were gone, the Devil grumbled unhappily. Still, he obeyed her command. He probably sensed that he had already pushed his luck enough with her for one night. With a wave of his hand, all of the flames that lingered around Torcello disappeared. Buildings that had been destroyed in the Onemdi's attack were repaired. Even the jam-filled crates that Aella had sent him flying into were put back together and stacked neatly in their corner. Everything, for all intents and purposes, was as it had appeared prior to the Devil's appearance earlier that evening.

The only remaining evidence of the battle was the burn on my side and the tremors wracking my body.

"Keep that as a souvenir," he hissed snidely, gesturing toward my arm, which was still wrapped protectively around my ribs. Evidently, even the goddess of the dead couldn't intimidate the vengefulness out of the Devil.

With one final look of disgust and anger, the Devil, too, swept away through the portal. Then, the fiery doorway to Hell snapped shut, and all was quiet.

CHAPTER NINETEEN

Torcello was silent, save for the babbling water in the canal. It was as though none of the events of the past few hours had happened. I might have even believed that, if it weren't for the flaring pain in my side, my uncontrollable shaking, and my aching head.

"Well, that was interesting," Leo commented.

"That's the understatement of the century," Nina quipped.

Ignoring her, Leo continued enthusiastically, "Hey, who knew the little tyke could pack such a punch?" He ruffled Aella's hair. The young girl giggled under the attention.

"Yeah, you never told us she was a Sylph," Matteo said, speaking for the first time since I collapsed.

"We didn't know," Arun admitted with a shrug, his

bow hanging limply in his hand as he stared wide-eyed at his sister. "She's technically our half-sister—same mother, different fathers. All three of us inherited our mother's goddess blood. We didn't know Aella's father was a Voktere, though."

"Part goddess, part Voktere..." Leo shook his head. "Talk about a mini powerhouse!"

"How long have you had your powers?" Janara asked, finally lowering her own bow as well.

"I don't know," Aella shrugged. "Since I got captured, I guess. I just got so angry with them when they took me—the next thing I knew, I was blowing them all over. They ended up locking me in a room because I caused a hurricane."

You could have heard a pin drop as we all gaped at Aella. Then, Janara started to laugh. That captured our attention—it was almost more shocking than the fact that Aella was a Sylph. With the exception of Arun, none of us had ever heard Janara laugh. It was a melodic sound, almost like chimes—both beautiful and sincere.

Arun was the first to recover from his astonishment, his light chuckles mingling with his sister's. Leo, Nina, and Elena joined in shortly after. Aella bobbed happily as she watched the group, glad to be a source of amusement. Matteo grinned broadly, and even I managed a tiny smile. It was bizarre—the eight of us laughing and smiling together only minutes after fighting the Devil and his army of demons, rescuing Aella from the depths of Hell, and facing Hela. Whether our mirth was from Aella's confession, Janara's rare laughter, or the immense relief that we had all survived—and successfully averted—the crisis on Torcello... I wasn't sure.

Gradually, our chuckles died away, leaving us in the comfortable stillness of the night.

"Well, I don't know about all of you, but I can honestly say that I've had enough adventure for one day," Leo stated, draping an arm around Nina's shoulders. "How about we all go home?"

"I'm all for that," Nina chirped. "Elena, you can stay with us for the night, if you'd like."

"That would be wonderful, merci," she replied. Nina nodded, then turned her attention to me.

"Kat, are you alright?"

She watched in concern as Matteo helped me to my feet. A wave of dizziness overcame me as I stood upright, and I swayed precariously, grasping at Matteo's arm to steady myself. He tightened the arm that he had slipped around my waist, his hand careful of the burns marring my side.

"Kat?" Matteo's soft question drew my eyes to his, and I frowned at the worried crease in his brow.

"I'm alright," I said breathlessly, giving Matteo's arm a reassuring pat. As the dizziness faded, I gave a small, albeit strained, smile. Softly, I repeated, "I'm alright."

I was grateful that Matteo didn't press the issue, even though I knew he could feel my pain through our bond. Instead, he simply pulled me closer to him. And when I sagged bonelessly against him, he said nothing. He only shifted his arm so that he could support more of my weight.

"I think we could all use some rest and first aid," Janara stated. It was true that I was in the worst shape out of all of them, but everyone else had also sustained various cuts, bruises, and burns during the night's events.

"I agree," Matteo nodded, keeping his eyes on me. "Let's go home." I nodded feebly beside him. Walking—or, in my case, limping—slowly along the canal path, the eight of us made our way back toward the docking point at the far end of Torcello. Climbing aboard the waiting vaporetto, we soon found ourselves zipping rapidly out into the Adriatic. All of us sat silently as the vessel rose and dipped with the waves, watching as the dark silhouette of Torcello faded into the distance.

Exhaustion and injury had brought us all to the flat that Nina and I shared—for although it was smaller than Matteo and Leo's, it was significantly closer to the main canal where we had docked. I nearly sobbed in relief when we set foot in it. The constant movement of the boat, followed by our trek between the canal and the apartment had made my injured side protest loudly. Combined with the lingering effects of whatever Hela's guard had hit me with, the sheer stress from everything that had happened that night, and the comforting familiarity of home—a home I thought only a few hours ago that I might never see again—I was also feeling rather emotional. My nerves were frayed, and my throat burned with restrained sobs. Of course, I still had enough presence of mind to be frustrated by my sentimentality, which only made the sting of tears behind my eyes worse.

As soon as the eight of us crossed the threshold, we dispersed to different areas of the apartment so that we could have a bit of privacy in which to tend our wounds and find some much-needed solitude.

Nina, endlessly selfless, gave her own bedroom to Elena for the night. After some brief protestations from Elena that such an offer was far too generous and would be an imposition, she graciously accepted. Still spewing thanks that alternated between French, Italian, and English, she made her way to Nina's room and relegated herself to its confines for the rest of the night.

I likewise offered up my room so that Aella could have a bed in which to sleep. Having fallen asleep on the trip back to Murano, the small Sylph was carried into the bedroom by her older brother. She had her head nestled into the crook of his neck as she dozed. Janara trailed close behind them, smiling fondly at the sight despite the fatigue in her eyes.

Leo ushered Nina into the living room. Ever since we had docked on Murano, she had seemed rather dazed; but trying to figure out why—let alone inquire about it—required far more effort and energy than I was currently capable of expending. My mind was functioning like a sloth, and in its sluggishness, I could barely even keep track of what was happening to *me* right now, never mind other people.

Speaking of which...

When had I sat down?

I didn't remember sitting at the kitchen table, and now, the fact that I was nestled into one of our old wooden chairs was of the utmost interest to me. My hand, too, seemed peculiarly fascinating. It had previously been perched on Matteo's arm, but was now resting on the table. The wood was hard and cold—not at all like Matteo. For some inexplicable reason, I was deeply troubled by the change.

Where *was* Matteo anyway? Hadn't he just been here? Where did he go?

I thought I recalled a whispered, "I'll be right back."

Perhaps there was also a hand on my shoulder, a gentle squeeze that accompanied the words. But it was all extraordinarily hazy, so I couldn't make heads nor tails of it. Instead, my brain ignored it, reverting back to old fears—things that had been pounded into it for so long throughout my youth that they were now second nature.

Had Matteo left? Did he finally come to his senses and recognize the impossibility of our relationship? Was he afraid of me now that he had seen my powers in action? Had he gotten sick of me for being such a burden tonight? Had I been too weak during the battle?

"You are the strongest person I know," came the soft, but firm answer from behind me. I spun around to look at Matteo, staring blankly at him. *Oh, wait... had I said all of that out loud? Oops.* "I would never think you weak *or* a burden, and I never want you to think that of yourself, either." A couple of blinks was my only response.

He seemed to realize that my mind was far too foggy to be having deep, meaningful conversations at the present moment. So, sighing tiredly, he sank down in the chair next to me, placing a familiar white box on the table in front of him. A first aid kit, my brain helpfully supplied. Ah, so apparently it was willing to function just enough to process *that*.

"You and I are going to have a long conversation about everything you just said. Not right now," he quickly added, seeing my face scrunch up at the thought. "But in a few days, when you're a bit more coherent and no longer collapsing from pain and exhaustion and whatever spell it was that Hela's guard hit you with. Then, and *only then*, will we have this discussion. I refuse to let you continue wandering around with such fears and insecurities."

Tempering his voice, he continued, "But for the time being, we need to take care of your injuries. Are you alright with that?"

I nodded, confused as to why I wouldn't be. Somewhere in the back of my mind, the ghost of a memory—an angry *Don't touch me!*—drifted just below the surface, but its wispy presence was gone before I could grasp it.

"Grazie," he said. Again, I had no idea why he would be thanking me for allowing him to help me—but if it made his eyes dance with joy and the worry lines on his face smooth out with relief the way they were doing now, then I wasn't going to question it.

I watched as Matteo rummaged around in the first aid kit, pulling various jars, bottles, and bandages from the box. Despite the determined set of his features, he looked drained of all energy.

"You don't have to do this, you know," I said quietly. "You're tired. I can see it. I can *feel* it."

"I know I don't have to, but I want to." Matteo gave me a warm smile, then abandoned his chair, moving to kneel by my side. His fingers lightly brushed over my burned skin, gently probing the injured area as he inspected it. He was barely even touching me, yet it felt like I was being jabbed with a hot poker. Then there was a sharp tug, and I hissed at the pain.

"I'm sorry," he murmured, wincing in sympathy. "But there are pieces of your shirt stuck to the skin. I have to get them out, otherwise they'll infect the wound. I'm being as gentle as I possibly can."

I nodded once, knowing he wasn't intentionally trying to hurt me. Still, the feel of the fabric pulling at my burned, oozing flesh as it was removed was a special kind of torture. My hands balled into fists, my nails digging into my palms as I tried to breathe through the pain.

Fortunately, cleaning out the wound didn't take long. After several minutes, Matteo sat back on his heels, a small pile of the bloodied shreds of my shirt on the table next to him.

"Well, it looks like I got all the pieces out," he declared, his eyes scanning the injury in a final once-over. "Now, for the hard part." I looked over at him sharply, dread pooling in my stomach. I must have looked as horrified as I felt, because he gave me an apologetic expression. "I have to disinfect it."

"Matteo—"

"Kat, I'm sorry, but it has to be done. I don't want it to get infected."

I sighed, nodding in acceptance. Logically, I knew he was right—disinfecting had to happen. Still... the thought of it made me cringe. I remembered all of the times that I received scrapes and cuts as a young girl—falling off my bike, tripping into my mother's rose bush, tumbling off a playground set, my sister and I trying to ice skate using our powers in the middle of summer. Each time, my parents had poured disinfectant on the injuries, and it always stung so harshly that it brought tears to my eyes. And those had been small wounds. This was a massive burn covering half my torso. I didn't even want to think about how much this was going to hurt.

As it turned out, I didn't have to think about it. A second later, something wet and cold was pressing against my side, and the skin beneath it erupted in pain. For a brief moment, I vaguely wondered if this was what calves felt like when being branded with an iron. The thought was quickly chased from my mind though by the sheer agony that consumed my entire being. I squeezed my eyes shut, clutching at the edge of the table with a white-knuckled grip, and grinding my teeth together to prevent myself from crying out. I couldn't, however, stop the occasional whimper that tore from my throat against my will.

As more disinfectant was dabbed on the irritated skin, a repeated chorus of murmured apologies tumbled from Matteo's lips. His voice was strained, and even through the cloud of nearly debilitating stinging and throbbing, I could feel our bond buzzing with the distress that he felt at causing me pain. I knew that he was only trying to help me, and I desperately wanted to reassure him of that—but I also knew that if I opened my mouth now, a scream was sure to come out instead. And somehow, I didn't think that would help to ease Matteo's worries.

After what felt like an eternity, Matteo finally finished disinfecting the burn. Screwing the cap back on the bottle, he set it back on the table.

"There," he announced, sounding just as relieved as I felt. "The worst part is over."

I released a harsh exhale, loosening my grip on the table.

"Just breathe," Matteo encouraged softly. "In and out. That's it." I followed Matteo's instructions, glad to have something other than pain to focus on. Inhaling several deep breaths and then releasing them slowly, the fire that felt like it was consuming my side gradually dissipated. It was replaced by an uncomfortable tingling—and although it still hurt, it was at least more bearable than before.

"I'm just going to put some burn salve on it, and then

I can bandage it."

I gave Matteo a wary look, but said nothing.

"Are you alright?" he asked. "You look a bit pale."

"I'm fine," I rasped. "Just... *please* go easy with it." I was rather ashamed by the pleading tone of my voice, but at this point, everything hurt too much for me to care.

"Amore mio, I promise I will." He leaned forward, placing a tender kiss on my head. "I'm so sorry I hurt you, but I swear I was being as gentle as I could be. You don't need to worry, though—the rest won't hurt as much." At my look of skepticism, he added, "Trust me, I've burned myself enough times with my powers to know how all of this feels."

Unscrewing a small white jar, he shoved his fingers into the contents, scooping out a liberal amount of the cream inside. I tensed, biting my bottom lip and closing my eyes as I waited for the onset of more pain.

When the salve touched my skin, I flinched at the extreme cold of it. It quickly warmed with my body temperature though as Matteo delicately applied it to the injured area. Other than the initial chill of each new glob of the aloe cream, there was no discomfort or pain. Every now and then, I experienced a slight twinge as the raw skin moved beneath his ministrations, but it was barely even noticeable. Soon, I felt myself relaxing, the cold of the cream soothing against the heat of the burn.

"It helps, doesn't it?" I could hear the smile in Matteo's voice without even needing to look at him. I nodded in agreement, closing my eyes in relief as the pain ebbed away. "Yes, I always thought so, too."

Once the wound was coated with cream, Matteo covered it with a large wad of protective gauze, which he secured in place with a white cloth bandage.

"Voila," he stated with a dramatic flourish as he finished tying the bandage in place. "All done."

I placed a hand over the cloth binding, experimenting with small movements. There was still a dull ache if I shifted at certain angles, but overall, I wasn't in even half of the pain that I was before.

"It feels much better," I confirmed, offering him a smile. "Grazie mille."

"I'm glad to hear it," he responded cheerily. "Are you hurt anywhere else?"

"No," I shook my head. "At least, I don't think so."

Matteo raised an eyebrow at me.

"When Hela's guard hit me with... well, whatever it was she shot me with, it did something weird to my head."

"What do you mean?"

I shrugged. "It felt like a migraine, but worse. Much worse."

"Does your head still hurt?"

"Not anymore. My mind does feel a bit sluggish, though. My thoughts feel kind of hazy."

"Hmm," he hummed thoughtfully. He placed light fingers against my temples, rubbing soothing circles over the pressure points and relieving some of the lingering headache. Tilting my head slightly to one side, then the other, Matteo examined it with his eyes while his fingers traveled across my face and scalp, probing for signs of injury. When he found none, he frowned.

"I can't find any physical injuries. Do you have any other symptoms other than the fogginess?"

"No. Just a tiny headache, but it's much better than it was."

Matteo was silent for a moment, observing me. "I don't know what she hit you with," he stated, concern written clearly across his face. "But physically, there seem to be no effects. And since your headache is going away, I'm assuming that whatever that spell did to you is wearing off. I think with a little sleep, you should be as good as new."

"Mmm, sleep sounds good." Now that he mentioned it, I felt utterly exhausted. My limbs were heavy, and my eyes drooping against my will.

"Are you sure you're alright?" Matteo inquired. A warm tingle—what I now recognized as Matteo's signature in our bond—flowed through my system, carrying with it both concern and comfort. I gave myself a small shake, trying to wake myself just long enough for the one final task I wanted to accomplish tonight.

"I'm fine," I reassured him, placing my hand over his and giving it a squeeze. "Like you said, it's nothing a little sleep won't fix. But first—" I reached for the first aid kit, dragging it to my side of the table. "It's my turn to help you."

"Kat, you don't have to do that," he protested.

"I know, but I want to." I tossed his words back at him, which earned me an incredibly soft look of fondness. Offering him an affectionate smile, I set to work cleaning, disinfecting, and bandaging his injuries—a cut on his cheek, a small burn on his forearm, scrapes on his hands. Tending to his wounds was almost therapeutic, in a way. It required my total attention, yet very little thought. In such circumstances, my mind couldn't wander—not that it could do much wandering in its current condition anyway. More importantly, caring for Matteo gave me a physical reminder that he was alive and well—that he truly was sitting in front of me, safe and sound. I hadn't lost him tonight. That thought alone caused tears of relief and gratitude to fill my eyes.

"There," I announced, clearing my throat against the emotion choking it as I applied the last bandage to his hand. "Fato."

"Grazie," he murmured, his eyes shining with warmth. I nodded mutely in response, then started packing the assemblage of supplies back into the box. I had just returned the gauze and bandages to the kit when my movements were stopped by one of Matteo's hands covering my own.

"Are you alright?"

"Huh?" I glanced up at Matteo, confused. Hadn't he already asked me that? I could've sworn I answered that question. "Yes, of course. You just took care of my injuries—"

"I didn't mean physically," he clarified. At my perplexed look, he elaborated. "I remember what you said about how you feel about using your powers, especially when it comes to making shields. Tonight, you used your powers offensively *and* made a shield—a rather impressive one, I might add. I just want to make sure you're okay with all of that."

"Oh," I mumbled, fixating my attention on our joined hands. I hadn't thought about that. But now that I had…

"Yeah, I am actually." I covered his hand with my own so that it was sandwiched between my palms. "Before all of this—before our soulbond—I saw my powers as something bad. To me, they were the embodiment of the monster I had been taught to believe I was. But tonight, when I had no choice but to use my powers against the forces of Hell in order to protect Venice, my friends, you?" I shrugged. "It showed me that it's not my powers who define me at all. It's actually the other way around. The way I *choose* to use my powers is all that matters. And tonight, I saw all the good things that my powers are capable of." I paused, huffing out a short laugh. "Turns out Janara was right about that."

Matteo positively beamed at my words. His face broke into a huge smile that was so bright it could have lit up a dark room. He raised one of my hands to his lips, brushing a soft kiss against my bruised knuckles in a show of affection that made my heart swell.

"I was so afraid that I would lose you tonight," I confessed, my voice barely audible. He squeezed my hand, tangling our fingers together. Our soulbonds rested against each other, thrumming in contentment at the close contact.

"But you didn't. I'm right here," he reminded me. "And so are you."

I nodded, recognizing his words for what they were— a reassurance to himself that I, too, had survived. He had feared losing me just as much as I had feared losing him, and now that it was all over, the reality was finally sinking in—we were both still here, we were both still alive...

We were both still *together*.

We stayed like that for several minutes, simply holding on to each other and relishing in our closeness. It was a period of deep, meaningful silence, our hearts beating in unison and our bond practically vibrating with satisfaction.

Until I yawned—loudly. It came out of nowhere, and I

flushed in embarrassment. Matteo chuckled.

"I think that's our cue that we should get some sleep."

"Yeah, that's probably a good idea," I agreed, with a shy twitch of my lips.

"Come," he said, standing from his chair and tugging me up with him. My limbs felt boneless, my eyes heavy. I allowed Matteo to lead me into the den, where Leo and Nina were curled up in the two armchairs that faced each other across the coffee table. They both seemed to be fast asleep—Nina's breathing was heavy, but steady from within her cocoon of blankets; and Leo was snoring softly, his head pillowed on his folded arms.

Matteo ushered me to the couch, easily helping me to lay down on it. Careful of my side, he maneuvered me so that I was resting comfortably. As soon as my head hit the cushioned arm of the sofa, my eyes started to drift shut. There was a soft rustling sound, but I couldn't quite make out what it was as I drifted in the void between wakefulness and repose. Something warm and soft was draped over my body, and I snuggled into it happily. A soft kiss was placed on the top of my head.

"Matteo?" I mumbled sleepily.

"Shh, I'm here, amore mio—and I always will be." I made a contented sound, burrowing deeper into the blanket covering me. "Sogni d'oro."

There were fingers combing softly through my hair, and a barely audible humming near my ear that gradually lulled me to sleep. The sound was beautiful and soothing, the tune familiar—but before I could grasp at the memory, the dark fingers of sleep closed around me, and I knew no more.

CHAPTER TWENTY

Thump, thump. Bang. Screeech.

"Shhh!"

I blinked my eyes open. There was a moment of confusion that always abounds from waking up in a different place than usual. But as my eyes flitted over my surroundings, my brain rapidly calculated my location—dark green sofa, mint-colored fleece blanket, cluttered coffee table, odd aroma of old books and honey.

Home.

"You have to be quiet—you'll wake Kat!"

Well, if nothing else, that voice definitely verified my location.

I pushed myself into a sitting position, wincing as the burn on my side protested at the sudden movement.

"Sorry!" came the muffled reply. "But the chair attacked me!"

"Leo," a different voice groaned, clearly exasperated. I smirked, stifling a chuckle. This sounded too good to miss.

Shoving the blanket off of myself, I made my way to the kitchen. Nina had a hand in her hair, looking like she couldn't decide whether to be frustrated or entertained. Matteo was leaning back in his chair, shaking his head in disbelief at his brother. And Leo...

Well, Leo had one foot stuck between the stretcher bars joining two of the chair legs, and a small suitcase mysteriously caught on both the trapped foot and the chair. How he had even managed to get himself into such a predicament—let alone keep himself upright throughout it—I wasn't sure. It was, however, rather humorous, and I raised an eyebrow, eager to see how this was all going to play out.

At that moment, Leo must have sensed my presence in the room, because his eyes snapped up to stare at me. As soon as he saw me, his face morphed into an expression of guilt and horror.

"Kat, I am *so sorry* that I woke you up. I really didn't mean to!" His apology was interspersed by him hopping around on his free foot, trying to maintain his balance. I bit the inside of my cheek to prevent myself from laughing. Leo looked sincerely troubled by the thought that he had disturbed my rest, and I had no desire to worsen his guilt. Besides, it seemed he was having enough issues in his losing battle with the chair—he didn't need people laughing at him for it. At least, not right now. Later? Definitely.

"It's alright, Leo," I assured him. Somehow, that only seemed to increase his remorse, and his face twisted in grief. He looked like a child who was being reprimanded by his mother. Taking pity on him, I tried a different approach. "You didn't wake me," I fibbed easily. "I was already awake."

Matteo stood from his place at the table, walking over to greet me. He slipped an arm around my waist, his hand resting carefully below where the burn on my ribcage was located.

"Liar," he whispered in my ear, though there was no bite in his tone. Instead, he sounded almost fond. His eyes twinkled and his mouth twitched into a crooked smile. I grinned at him, and he placed a kiss on my head.

"Buongiorno, Kat!" Nina chirped, smacking Leo's arm as she strolled past him with a cup of tea. She offered me the steaming cup, which I accepted gratefully. "How are you feeling?"

"Much better than yesterday. And you?"

"Oh, I'm fine. I was exhausted last night, but I feel fantastic now."

"That's great," I responded, taking a sip of the tea. My eyes fell back on Leo, who was now bent over the chair at an awkward angle, trying to extricate himself from it. "So, uh, how exactly did this situation come about?" I asked, waving vaguely at the scene in front of us with my hand.

"Oh, that." Nina rolled her eyes. "Leo and I were supposed to take Elena to the airport today—her flight back to France leaves early this afternoon. But when we woke up this morning, she asked us if we wanted to go with her. Leo, of course, said yes immediately. I think he was packing his suitcase before she had even finished asking the question."

"Hey, I waited until she was done talking," Leo protested, hopping around some more as he jiggled his foot, the chair banging loudly on the floor with the movement. Nina shook her head, sighing.

"Anyway, I agreed to go as well. I mean, it's France—how could I say no?"

"*You* agreed to go to France?" I asked incredulously. "Alright, who are you and what have you done with my best friend?"

Nina smiled sheepishly, scuffing at the tiled floor with the toe of her shoe. "Well, the past few weeks have shown me that maybe adventures outside of books aren't all that bad."

I grinned, catching the glance she shot at Leo out of the corner of her eye.

"That, and she and I get to spend some more time together," Leo declared, frowning down at the chair as though it had personally offended him. "Turns out, she's not so bad... and neither are her books." He bounced several times, stumbling around in a circle as he wiggled his foot some more, pushing at the suitcase until it finally slid free. He toppled over onto the floor with a proud, "Aha!"

Nina watched the scene with wide eyes, embarrassment and horror battling for control of her features.

"Yeah," Nina said slowly. "On second thought, maybe I should rethink this trip..."

Leo spluttered out an undignified sound of offense.

"Don't you dare!"

She chuckled, kneeling beside him to help remove his foot from the final rung of the chair. Once it was free, she sat back on her heels and sighed.

"Well, if you insist." Then, with a feigned shrug of indifference, she added, "After all, someone has to keep you out of trouble." Leo glowered at her grumpily.

"She's got you there," Matteo commented, earning an even darker scowl from his younger sibling.

"I'm sure it will be nice for you two to go to France and actually enjoy it this time, instead of being on a life-or-death mission," I offered.

"Actually, you both could come, too." We turned toward Elena, who had just wandered into the kitchen carrying a bag over her shoulder. She dropped it on the chair beside the door, then spun to face us. "My invitation is not limited only to Leo and Nina. You're *all* welcome to visit with me for a while—you, Matteo, Janara, Arun, Aella."

"That's really sweet of you, but that's a lot of people to have staying with you," I pointed out. "We might get in your way. And besides, you barely even know us."

"I'm not concerned about the number of people. My house isn't large, by any means—but it's big enough that we could all stay there comfortably. And, in all honesty, it would be nice to have some company for a while. As far as not knowing you..." she shrugged. "Last night, we saved Venice from the Devil, fought off fire demons from Hell, and stood up to the Goddess of Death herself. I think I know you all as well as I need to."

I snorted. "Well, I guess you have a point at that." I turned to Matteo. "What do you think? I've always wanted to see France."

"I already checked with Carlo," Leo chimed in. "He said we can take as much time off as we want—especially since neither of us has taken a day off since we started working there."

"It would be nice for everyone to get away from Venice

for a little while—get some distance from all that has happened the past few weeks," Elena added.

"She's right," Nina agreed.

"Well, then, how can I say no?" Matteo pulled me closer. "When do we leave?"

I squealed happily, throwing my arms around his neck. The movement jostled my side, and I sucked in a breath.

"Easy," Matteo murmured. "You're still healing."

I nodded, but despite the pain, I couldn't keep the smile from my face.

"Merveilleux!" Elena clapped her hands together in delight just as Leo gave a hoot of glee.

"What's all the excitement about?" came Janara's voice as she emerged from the hall, followed closely by Arun and a bleary-eyed Aella.

"We're all going to France!" Nina gleefully exclaimed.

"Elena is going back to France today, and she invited all of us—including the three of you—to stay with her for a couple of weeks," I explained.

"Really?"

"Yes," Elena nodded. "I'd love for you all to come."

"That's extremely generous of you," Janara stated. "But I think we'll take a rain check. Considering we were here in Venice on holiday, I'd say our track record with visiting new places isn't all that great right now. I think going home for the rest of our holiday would be safer."

"Yeah, home sounds good," Arun agreed.

"Perhaps another time then," Elena responded in understanding.

"That would be lovely, thank you," Janara replied with a smile.

"So, the three of you are heading back to London?" I

asked Janara, unable to keep the hint of sadness from my voice.

"Yes," she answered somewhat apologetically as Arun moved past her to sit at the table, settling Aella in his lap. "We leave today. Our flight is at one. I know it's a bit soon, but it was the only flight out that we could get."

"Our flight leaves at the same time," Elena commented. "We can head to the airport together."

"In the meantime, we still have a couple of hours together," Leo pointed out. "And we'll just have to make the most of it."

"How about some tea?" Nina asked Janara, who was currently the only person in the room without a cup of the hot liquid.

"I'm British," Janara said matter-of-factly. "Do you even need to ask?"

Nina laughed. "I guess not." Then, turning to one of the cabinets, she added, "Sit, I'll get you a cup."

And for the next two hours, the kitchen was filled only with the sounds of clinking china, friendly chatter, and hearty laughter.

Our eight-person group was successfully checked through security and maneuvering down the long, packed corridors of the airport. It was remarkable that we had actually arrived early—for a short while, we didn't even think we would get to the airport at all. Yes, Matteo and I had to scramble to pack, considering we didn't even know we were going to France until *today*. But the tardiness of our little unit wasn't *our* fault. It was, surprisingly—or perhaps unsurprisingly, considering the events of that morning—Leo's.

As it turned out, entrusting plane tickets to a person who had literally gotten himself *stuck in a chair* was not the brightest idea that any of us had ever had. Oh, Janara, Arun, and Aella were fine, since Janara was the one responsible for holding their tickets. But Elena, Matteo, Leo, Nina, and I were out of luck. Within five minutes of Leo convincing us that he should be the "ticket-keeper," the tickets had vanished.

Fortunately, after a half-hour of searching for the lost tickets, Nina found them in the fruit bowl. None of us even bothered to ask how they had gotten there. We didn't want to know.

Needless to say, Leo wasn't allowed to touch the tickets again until we were at the check-in counter. Matteo held onto them instead.

Two cabs, a chaotic baggage check-in, and eight individual security scans later, we were all united once more, searching for our respective gates with an impressive amount of time to spare.

"Well, this is us," Janara stated, gesturing to the gate just to our right. Then, turning to face us, she said, "Thank you—all of you—for what you did for Aella... for *us*."

"Yeah, thanks," Arun echoed, nodding emphatically.

"We'd do it again in a heartbeat," Nina answered. "We owe you our thanks as well, for helping to save Venice."

"All in a day's work," Arun retorted with a good-natured wink.

"Don't be strangers," Leo chimed in, shaking hands with Janara and Arun and ruffling Aella's hair.

"We won't be," Arun assured. "And if any of you are ever in London, look us up."

"Will do," Leo promised.

"Emiliano Beretti, viene al'uscita d'imbarco numero nove. Noi abbiamo trovato il Suo biglietto aereo. Ancora, Emiliano Beretti, viene al'uscita d'imbarco numero nove, per favore."

As soon as the announcement had finished, Leo began shoving his hands into his pockets, his eyes wide as he frantically searched for the lost ticket. Coming up empty-handed, he scratched his head.

"Huh, I guess I really did lose it. At least they found it!" With that, he bounded away in the direction of gate nine.

"I'm never traveling with him again," Matteo mumbled in my ear, and I barked out a laugh.

"I'd better go with him," Nina decided, watching Leo's form retreating down the corridor. "With the way his day's going, he'll probably lose the ticket again before he even gets back."

"Yeah, or he'll get on the wrong plane," Arun snickered.

"Oh no," Nina groaned, her eyes growing round like saucers as that very real possibility hit her. Turning and racing down the long hall after Leo, she called after him, "Leo, wait!"

No sooner had Nina disappeared out of earshot, then we all burst out laughing. We couldn't help it. It was simply too funny.

"Well," Elena said once she had recovered, swiping at the tears that had swelled in her eyes with her laughter. "I'm going to go find our gate and get settled."

Janara nodded, adding a heartfelt, "Thank you, again."

"We'll be right there," I told Elena. She gave a final wave, and disappeared down the corridor in the same direction as Nina and Leo.

"So, it's back to London for the three of you," I stated lamely after a moment of awkward silence. I had never been great with goodbyes.

"Yeah," Janara responded. From the soft look she was giving me, she seemed to understand my discomfort.

"Well, I guess we should be on our way, too—"

"Wait, I have something for you!" chirped Aella. She pranced forward, pulling something from her pocket. She stared up at me for a moment, then down at the object in her hands, and then back up at me. "Come down here, please," she demanded lightly. "I'm not that tall yet."

"Aella," Janara said warningly. I merely chuckled, obeying the Sylph's command. She reached up, sliding something over my neck. It was a necklace. The piece of jewelry was beaded, just like my kedja had been—but instead of being a unified ice blue, it consisted of alternating patterns of navy blue and gold. In the center, lying right over the small indent between my collarbone was a single pale bead, slightly larger than the others, that glistened brightly even in the dim airport fluorescents. My fingers traced it reverently, and something oddly familiar tingled through me.

"You lost your necklace trying to protect me, so I wanted to give you a new one. Arun and Janara helped me make it," Aella declared proudly. "J told me that your other necklace wasn't good for you, but this one is different. It's a... skjold?" She experimented with the word, and beamed when Janara nodded her approval. "If you're ever in danger, this will protect you." She tapped the pale blue bead gently. "I'm not really sure how it works—Janara explained it to me, but it was really confusing and I got bored." She shrugged.

"You're having a bad influence on her," Janara said, pinning Arun with narrowed eyes.

"Me? A bad influence?" Arun replied innocently. "Never." He gave Aella a wink and a nudge with his elbow though, which made Janara roll her eyes.

"Children," she muttered exasperatedly.

"I put my powers into it," Aella continued brightly, practically dancing where she stood as she eyed the necklace. "So, it will probably blow things over or something."

"Well, if it has your powers in it, then it is surely a formidable force," I responded seriously. Kneeling down, I wrapped her in a hug. "Thank you."

"Aella's powers are in the center bead," Janara explained. "The blue and gold beads represent me and Arun. There's nothing special about them though, since we don't have transferrable powers. If you are ever in extreme danger, that necklace will channel Aella's powers into you, allowing you to use them. Unfortunately, it only works once—but that should at least allow you enough time to escape. Plus, the skjold can only be removed by you, so you don't need to worry about anyone taking it from you."

"Thank you," I whispered, feeling overwhelmed by the kind gesture.

"It was nothing," Janara answered, brushing away my gratitude with a wave of her hand. "Hopefully, you'll never need to use it, and it can just serve as a small reminder of us."

"Il volo 2212 per Londra è in partenza."

"That's us," Arun stated. He looked at Matteo, extending his hand. "I'll see you around."

"Arrivederci," Matteo said, grasping his hand. "Grazie, ad entrambi."

"Bye, Matteo!" Aella launched herself at him, wrapping her arms around his waist.

"Ciao, Aella," he replied, patting her head. Then, holding her at arm's length, he poked her nose. "Be good."

She giggled. "I always am." Then, she flung herself at me. "Thanks for everything, Kat! I'm going to miss you."

"And I, you," I answered, embracing her petite frame. She pecked my cheek with a kiss, then returned to her brother's side.

"Bye, Kat," Arun said, stepping forward to hug me.

"Bye, Arun," I mumbled into his shoulder. Withdrawing just far enough to jab him in the chest, I added, "Don't drive Janara too crazy."

"I would never," I gasped in mock offense, feigning injury when Janara elbowed him in the ribs.

"Are you kidding? That's where he gets all his entertainment," she quipped.

"I'm wounded," he retorted with fake affront. "Come, Aella, let's go find our plane." Grabbing his sister's hand, they marched off towards the gate, Aella snickering the entire time.

"Come visit us!" she yelled back over her shoulder, giving a final wave before she and Arun disappeared into the crowds of people. Janara shook her head.

"No one told me that having a twin would be like taking care of a five-year-old."

"Don't worry, it seems to be a younger sibling trait, as well," Matteo commented dryly, jutting his head in the direction in which Leo had disappeared a few minutes earlier.

Janara snorted. "Seems like we've both got our work cut out for us."

"That, we do."

Janara grinned, but then her mood sobered once more. Her verdigris eyes flickered between me and Matteo.

"So, you never told me—what's the plan for the two of you now?" she asked.

"Well, I'm pretty sure I was promised an uninterrupted date if we all made it off of Torcello alive." I gave Matteo a playfully expectant look. He chuckled—a rich, deep sound that I absolutely loved.

"And I have every intention of keeping that promise," he assured, entwining our hands together. I smiled as he squeezed my fingers gently, then placed a light kiss on my forehead. Janara's lips twitched upward ever so slightly.

"I'm happy to hear that—for the both of you." Turning her attention to Matteo, she instructed seriously, "Take care of her."

"I will," he vowed.

"And you," she began, shifting her intense gaze to me. She stared hard at me, trying to convey a meaningful message with that single look. "Let him."

"I will," I echoed.

"Good." A huge smile spread across Janara's face, and she nodded. "Well, then, I leave you in each other's capable hands." She gave Matteo a pat on the shoulder, accompanied by a, "See you around, Fireball." Then, addressing me, she said softly, "Take care, Frosty." There was split-second of hesitation, but then she wrapped me in a tight hug.

"Ultima chiamata per il volo 2212 per Londra."

Stepping back, she settled her bag further up her shoulder. With one last glance that swirled with gratitude, approval, and sadness, Janara murmured a soft, "Ciao," before departing into the crowd.

I continued to stare after Janara long after she had disappeared onto the plane. Though I had only known her for a few weeks, she had quickly become one of my closest friends. From the very first day I met her, it had felt like we had known each other all our lives. There existed between us a level of understanding and comfort that was usually only ever attained by family. Even Arun and Aella had easily forced their way into my heart, occupying a space in my life that had once been reserved only for Del—and, many years later, Nina.

Maybe that's why it was so hard to see them go. In only a few weeks, they had blocked out the shadows cast on my soul by the family I lost nearly two decades ago. They were my siblings in arms, my kinfolk in heart, my family in soul. Somehow, in this vast expanse of time and space, we had found each other. And although distance might separate us, I knew that we would always remain close—tied together in spirit and supporting each other from afar, but forever ready to drop everything and go to the aid of the other if needed.

Still, I would miss them.

"Va bene?" Matteo questioned, raising his free hand to wipe away a few stray tears rolling down my cheek. I gave him a wet smile, leaning into his touch. A warm sensation, like soft sunlight, wafted through me. I closed my eyes, relishing in the feelings of comfort, support, and love that Matteo was projecting through our bond.

"Sì," I breathed. The reminder of Matteo's presence eased the pangs of sadness in my heart. Opening my eyes again, I allowed myself to get lost in the brown depths that always seemed to regard me with the utmost adoration.

Looking into his eyes was like gazing into the future—as though all of time was suddenly made visible to me, without constraints. Just like the first time I met him, Matteo was at the center of it all. He was the sun, keeping my orbit steady and my world bright and warm. He was my rock, giving me a firm and stable place to turn in times of confusion and uncertainty. He was my most trusted battle companion, my best friend, my soulmate.

Matteo was here—and he always would be. With that knowledge, I could face anything. Everything else would fall into place as the Norns decided.

"Il volo 0624 per Basilea è in partenza."

"We're being summoned," Matteo said, pointing in the direction of the speaker overhead. "Shall we?" He held out his arm. I giggled as I linked my own arm with his, nestling my hand in the crook of his elbow. "France awaits."

Indeed, it did. Well, France, *and* a date with the incredible man beside me.

Who knew what Colmar would bring? After all, it was known as the "Little Venice" of France. Most likely, there would be grand canals, elegant bridges, quaint squares...

And it would be fascinating to experience those popular Venetian traits through the lens of French culture.

Maybe Matteo and I would even venture out of Colmar to visit other parts of France—places like Paris, Versailles, or Nice. The options were endless. There was so much to do in France, so much see. But to be honest, so long as we were together, I didn't care all that much *what* we did.

There was one thing I was certain about, though.

If we happened to come across a bridge with a mythical past...

We absolutely were *not* going near it.

ABOUT ATMOSPHERE PRESS

Atmosphere Press is an independent, full-service publisher for excellent books in all genres and for all audiences. Learn more about what we do at atmospherepress.com.

We encourage you to check out some of Atmosphere's latest releases, which are available at Amazon.com and via order from your local bookstore:

Á Deux, a novel by Alexey L. Kovalev

What If It Were True?, a novel by Eileen Wesel

Solitario: The Lonely One, a novel by John Manuel

The Fourth Wall, a novel by Scott Petty

Knights of the Air: Book 1: Rage!, a novel by Iain Stewart

Heartheaded, a novel by Constantina Pappas

The Aquamarine Surfboard, a novel by Kellye Abernathy

A Very Fine House, a novel by Rose Molina

White Birch, a novel by Paul Edmund Lessard

Saigon, a novel by Ralph Pezzullo

Melody Knight: A Vampire's Tale, a novel by Tony Lindsay

Staged, a novel by Elsie G. Beya

A Grip of Trees, a novel by Phillip Erfan

ABOUT THE AUTHOR

Emily Ruhl was born and raised in the heart of New Jersey. A history buff at heart, she loves any opportunity that allows her to learn more about the past. In her spare time, she also enjoys studying different languages and cultures, exploring the great outdoors, and spending time with her family and friends. As a culmination of her fondness for folklore and all things Italian, *The Bonds Between Us* is Emily's debut novel.

Made in the USA
Middletown, DE
04 March 2022

62126383R00151